David P Reiter's poetry has been acclaimed in Australia, North America and Europe for many years. Winner of the Queensland Poetry Award in 1989, he was commended for the same award in 1994. His fourth book, **Hemingway in Spain and Selected Poems**, was shortlisted for the John Bray Award at the 1998 Adelaide Festival. Frequently anthologised, he has toured his work several times in North America and will be touring Spain in 2000 with the support of the Australia Council and the University of Barcelona. Then he will assume a Leighton Studio Residency at the Banff Centre for the Arts, where he will prepare a hypermedia version of this book.

The **Literature Series** showcases the best in contemporary Australian writing available in digital as well as print form.

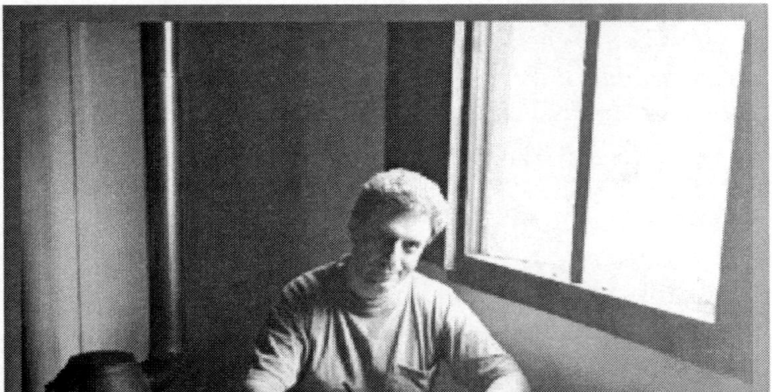

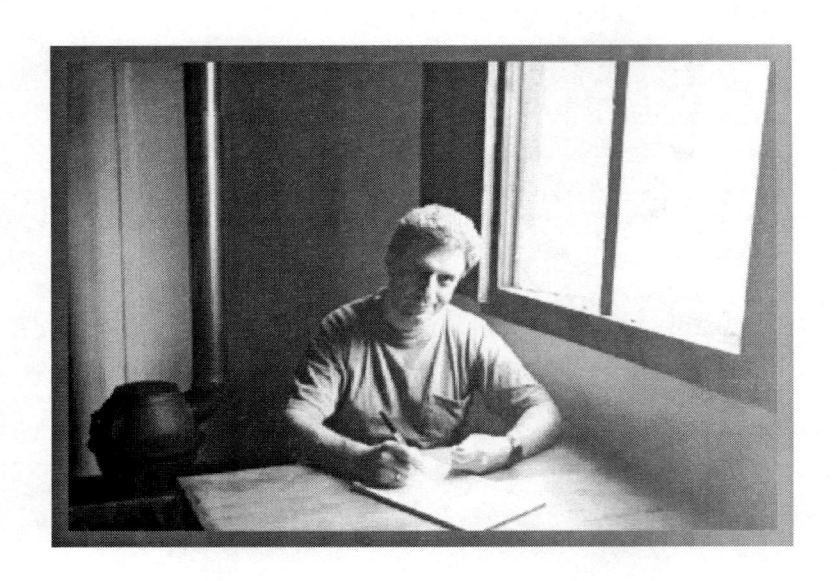

Letters We Never Sent

David P Reiter

Interactive Press
Literature Series

Interactive Press
an imprint of Interactive Publications
9 Kuhler Court
Carindale, Queensland
Australia 4152
sales@interpr.com.au
http://www.interpr.com.au

First published by Interactive Press, 2000
Copyright © David P Reiter, 2000

All rights reserved. Without limiting the rights under copyright reserved above, no part of this publication may be reproduced, stored in or introduced into a retrieval system, or transmitted, in any form or by any means (electronic, mechanical, photocopying recording or otherwise), without the prior written permission of both the copyright owner and the above publisher of this book.

Printed in 11/14 pt Book Antiqua, Georgia, Arial and Eurostyle on Lucida Handwriting. Produced in Australia.

National Library of Australia
Cataloguing-in-Publication data:

Reiter, David Philip, 1947 - .
Letters We Never Sent.
ISBN 1 876819 04 9.

I. Title. (Series: Literature Series (Carindale, Qld.)).

A823.3

This project was assisted by a grant from Arts Queensland, the Queensland Government's arts funding body.

For Paul and Vincent and those who keep the best stuff for themselves.

*I could have told you, Vincent,
the world was never meant
for one as beautiful as you.
        – Don McLean*

Acknowledgments

Many of these poems have appeared in earlier versions in the following publications, for which the author is grateful: Southerly, The Southern Review, Imago, Island, Northern Perspective, Idiom 23, Social Alternatives, Divan, The Age, The Canberra Times, Quadrant, Arc (Canada), Canadian Literature, Matrix (Canada), Fiddlehead (Canada), Ariga (Israel), Poetry Magazine (USA), Antipodes (USA), and Bogg (USA). Paul and Vincent, *a radio play adapted from sections of this book, was broadcast twice on Radio National, ABC.*

Thanks also to Peter Boyle and Philip Salom for their attentive reading of the work at the final boarding call.

Also by David P Reiter:

The Snow in Us (poems), Five Islands, 1989

Changing House (poems), Jacaranda, 1991

The Cave After Saltwater Tide, Penguin, 1994

Hemingway in Spain and Selected Poems, Interactive Press, 1997

Triangles, (short fiction), Interactive Press, 1999

Author's Note: The idea for this book came from the time I spent in Tahiti and the Cook Islands in 1994. My visit to the Gauguin Museum while in Tahiti and my discovery of *The Lagoon Is Lonely Now* by Ronald Symes, a journalist who spent many years living in the Cook Islands, prompted me to write a book that would counterpoint their experiences and impressions of island life with those of more familiar voices.

To assist the reader who wishes to keep track of the major voices, I have coded them by font as follows:

- the contemporary persona is in **Georgia**
- Gauguin's persona is in **Book Antiqua**
- Ronald Symes' persona is in **Arial**

The 'internet' sections, which also appear in Georgia font, provide a backdrop against which I was writing and a major sounding board for the themes raised in the major voice sections—the pleasurable voices/echoes you hear simply by being open to life as you render it on the page.

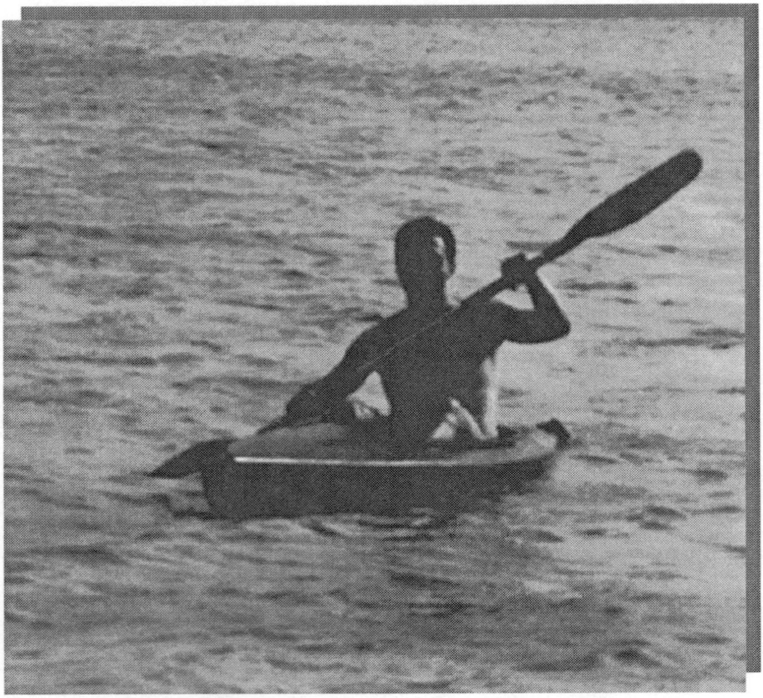

Contents

preludes 1

setting sail 6

the silence at night 14

give me that old time religion 22

intoxicants 33

shedding skin 44

déjà-vu 47

settling in 60

masks 65

lost in the translation 86

change of pace 95

soaring 105

reputations 113

keepsakes 122

twilight of the gods 132

preludes

The mind of Man is framed even like the breath
And harmony of music. There is a dark
Invisible workmanship that reconciles
Discordant elements, and makes them move
In one society.

    —Wordsworth

wandering jew
never at anchor
with the islands

in himself
afraid of boulders
abrading in the surf

on his hands and knees
he questions the potential
for green
checks for placentas taking
root in the niches

the hills are alive with prophesy
a sea eagle on currents of fire
plummets to pursue him through
canyons of woodchipped dreams
to the implacable dunes

a warning comes to him
on tongues of acrid surf
islands are too low to the sea
to embrace an art that seeks
more than palm fronds and mist

draped with uncertainty
we urge our dinghy to discover
a scenario of purpose
between the reefs
that channel of pure chance

then some invisible sandbar
gridlocks us in a deafening loop
chanting *black's a precursor to rebirth
so take a draught from this shell
and dive below your epilogue*

there's nothing to fear from coral
your fractures are nothing special
in this sector of bleeding colour
they only drown who renounce
the bloodline of speech

eyes closed you'll soon touch the floor
where your toes will mingle in the slurry
and you'll accept that breath was a mistake
and that only those who master
the epiphanies of death really matter

yet everything
in this tempest of sperm
around your head reminds you
of a niggling resurrection

seen from the sea the prospect is magnificent
shaded tints of green from beach to mountain-top
diverse with villages ridges glens and cascades
the peaks flinging their shadows down the valleys
the waterfalls flashing out in the sunlight
such enchantment breathes over the whole
it seems a fairy land all fresh and blooming
from the hand of the Creator [1]

preludes

I am a great artist and I know it

I came to Tahiti not
to reinvent it but to find
the savage under my skin
to barter my French civility for rags
of silence and in that interval
to surround myself with the chords
that must have struck Beethoven
after he sank into the isolation
of pure music.

I am tired of old planets.

At the end of this at the end
of effort I will be codified
by what I set out to seize
and it will not matter if no one
harbours my creations.

No man is an island
yet a painter must be that
and more —
a counterpoint of fluid and solid
intersection of thought and expression.

In that interrogation
he finds an essence that teases him
to voyage beyond the frame
to the sweet risks of the sentient
where each burst of colour
is one more corridor
between breath and death.

I too have a family
which I must never forget.

As long as you wait for me, Mette.[2]

the way the islands used to be
when the ships came in —
bronzed fellows bigger than me
strapping girls with moonlight teeth
and glossy black hair reaching
down to their midships

it's all gone now

currency
instead of gold [3]

Yet I want to believe that someone
out there is still listening
a sympathetic intelligence
of dancing light.

This is a tale of lagoons and islands
lonely reefs and villages drowsy
in the brilliant sun.

You write your impressions
even as the future unwrites you:

listen to a brown old man
rolling sennit on his bare wizened thigh
tossing his words carelessly
across the twilight
curve of a country road

soon
too soon
that old man will be you
though you'll remember
more of his reflection
than the mirror

preludes

you settle among the Takituma [4]
where they say the fishing's best
where there are seasons of *ka'i* [5]
you can scoop from the sand
with a coconut shell

you still conjure a winter wind
or nightingales trilling in the dusk
but safe in your sandcastle
you'll forget you've been
anywhere else.

setting sail

It's an unlikely gem —
Gill [6] called it a lovely spot
one of nature's fairest gardens
where he wished for man to be

an incarnation of love and holiness
not ignorant and vile and hateful
a worshipper of idols a slave
to carnality the devil himself.

The girls of Atiu were so warm
with their sex that Cook almost
forgot his marital vows.

He wrote in splotches
of their 'elegantly formed limbs'
fixing his nib
firmly on the page

while his spine stiffened
with saltspray.

Then in Tahiti
a girl with laughing brown eyes
cooked a dog specially for him
'I never ate sweeter meat'
he said and meant it.

She told him of her father's
father's father's father's father
and his crew who reached
the Antarctic in a canoe

setting sail

the fish were eager
for their nets but it was cold
so cold their coconut milk
slurried with ice before
it reached their tongues.
Cook had already missed
the peaks of Rarotonga
in the mist.

Bad luck.

My dearest Mette,

Such a grand dinner at the Café Voltaire —
so many painters and writers came out
to wish me well in my passage!

Mallarmé recited a poem for the toast
and all were inflamed by his words —
if I can deliver but *one-tenth*
of the promise he divined for me
over the next three years
it will be enough for us
to live securely.

Maybe then you'll understand
what kind of man fathered
your children.

　　—March 24, 1891, Paris

The crossing so far has been smooth
but I'm the only one who's actually
paid for his voyage.

The other passengers are either
servants of our kind government
or their wives and children
who've come along for the jaunt.

I should be more patient
with such decent people
who carry their family
everywhere they go.

It's not for me to criticise
them for their stiff collars
and mediocrity.

When we are at table
I do try to venture something
about the tenderness of the lamb

or the sweetness of the pudding
as you advised me but they seem
content just to chew so I'm left
to stare stupidly at the horizon
in the hope some porpoise might
disturb this canvas of dull waves.

It must be the length of my hair
that makes me a pariah now
or do they even know

of the name Gauguin?

    — May 4, 1891, Oceania

he said good-bye to his children
in slow-motion clips
a counter-rhythm to the idling car

two kittens grappled in the driveway
as he tried to make sense of it —
sign agent signifier agency signified

how to fabulate Australia

*an ad for Bacardi Rum insists
it's the world's biggest island
so what's cool for sexy Jamaica
must be cool for the suburbs too*

what if he'd said it with a Bacardi —
would that have made the message
any more tropical/topical for them?

*a satellite wakes in its slipstream
scratches at the electrons pocking
its skin before focussing its lens
on the continents/islands below*

he could have told them distances
are shrinking what with Concorde
faxes and e-mail and virtual reality

the idea/image of a father
can be as tangible as the father
himself *take this microchip*

*on your tongue as my flesh
press any key to commence
the program* once you scan in

the face it's easy to manipulate
the features and even put words
in his mouth through a emulator

with the flash of fibre optics
no daughter need be fatherless
no father needs to compromise

(instead they exchanged letters
report cards from grade to grade
the ledges the peaks the obligatory

photos of unshared and uncropped
experience absorbed
then concealed from scrutiny

he never admitted that children
could not be enough for him —
we must test the boundary

extend the grasp quicken the pace)
to *father* is the easy part of speech
an urgent thrust and withdrawal

whereas *fathering* is clay on soles
that refuses to dry and fall away
when he wants/needs to set sail

washed overboard? drowned?
no the artist's a fugitive
and proud of it

setting sail

the internet

playboy of the western world
hugh hefner
methodist child
methodist reborn before
the last stop on the train
to death

on the fast track between
his was everyman's grail
a surfeit of tits and bums

'power grace style...'
he had/lived it all

no island was safe from him
from the supersonic
parties the private
black jet

he never looked back at the pillar
of his first wife and their salty
children but monogamous again
he bronzed them on the lawn
of his playboy mansion
slightly out of focus
with a Circe who'd renounced
all urges to shipwreck

doting grandfather
slipping into the stale jacket
of yesterday's news

<HTML>

what's attractive about this network
of interchange is the loose *apparently*
unconstrained nature of social relations

an autonomy made possible by servers
who need no structured continuity
the sheer freedom of it all!

part of the tension for those not
intoxicated by this foreplay comes
from wondering who's excluded

just how useful *is* that deletion
of difference into a parlance
of universal consumption if you

don't have the credentials/credit
cards to be a player in the king's
software with the wild signifier

<HTML>

she's done her nails and lips
in peachy pink for the interview
to help her replay the instant

of mutilation before she tightened
the tourniquet around his bloodied
penis he trembling in the shower

at the coup de grâce when she
scissored off his pride and joy
and handed it to him (still hard)
like just one more cut lunch
but when she presses the button
the tape brings back the asylum

setting sail

where they locked her away
from her precious pink sheets
now *he's* the one who's cashing in

on the talk shows by telling how
the doctors stitched it back on
then washed and patted it dry

but the best part by far he says
(and I've never told anyone this)
was when I was standing there

in the shower with the blood
still throbbing down me legs
waiting on the ambulance

I lifted old dick to my lips
and gave him a nice big kiss —
I'd always wanted to do that

</HTML>

the silence at night

Almost a month since I landed
and my mind is still in a whirl.

When shall I be settled enough
to face a canvas again?

I've never felt a silence stranger
than this Tahitian night —
not a bird call dares disturb it
and if a leaf should faintly fall
it registers as nothing more
than a rustling of the mind.

There are those who will whisper
I've abandoned you, dear wife,
those who will never understand
how silence is a tonic to an artist
or how a passion can be enjoyed
without forcing it into stanzas.
They insist Paris is the centre
of all things, the Earth if not
the universe, they who think
they can find significance
in a road map or meaning
in the dregs of a teacup.

But without angle and distance
no perspectives are worthwhile.
What we worship as *civilisation*
is nothing more than a distraction
from the wild things that matter.
Why do we live if not to create?

the silence at night

Their pretences make me dizzy.
So I must clear my head of Pissarro [7]
and the alchemists who think beauty
is accreted by a dabbing of little dots.
I *will* find what I'm looking for here
once my sight adjusts to the light.

Tomorrow I swear I'll make a start!

After what felt to him an age almost
His wits returned and in a trembling tone
Rangi inquired if she was flesh or ghost
And, if of human kind, was she alone,
Whence she came and by what name she was known.
Struggling for words, 'I am,' she cried at last,
'Alone, Ake from Areora in the past.' [8]

Had his life come to this?
White-haired and stooped
Rangi still waiting for his Ake
the girl next door
the girl he was tattooed with/for
waist to thigh
the girl he married on a *marae*. [9]

Only he believed her alive now
though so many nights had past
the years were a ghost to him
a blur of words.
She'd wanted his child so badly
her mind ached with the absence
as she swept their cottage floor
as she waited for his canoe
to return from the reef each day

watching him by the dock
knee-deep in the red water
as he gutted his catch.
She saw anger in his knife
her own blood splattering
into the foam.

Bringing Turi to their cottage
had been a mistake —
he knew that now
as he hunched down in twilight
with a stick to prompt more letters
in the dirt outside their door.
Buxom Turi
he'd only meant her as company
to tease back Ake's laughter

He'd never touched her
though a man was permitted
a second wife for the sake of a son
even when Ake grew cold to him
and he tossed in his bed alone
with Turi just a whisper away.

The people searched for her
in the tangled undergrowth
from the *makatea* [10] at Konokonako
to the canoe landing at Matia
west to Oneroa east to Orovaru.
After they'd given up hope
they still tended his garden
so he'd always have a meal
when hunger forced him home.

He could have taken Turi then
she was the denouement/his due.

the silence at night

After so many months of grief
everyone said the gods
would smile on such a match
and she was always there waiting
at the blurred edge of his dreams.

It was a tiny *kura-moomoo* [11]
that came to him that noon
as he rested in the shade
of an old *tamanu* tree
that bid him follow deeper
and deeper into the confusion
of thorns on the *makatea*.
In the midst of it was a hole
and at the bottom of that
a cave where Ake sat
a blanched old woman
whispering on a stalagmite
to her broken limbs.

Back in their cottage
she told him of the voices
who woke her after her fall
who fetched her berries
who let the years ease by
like a pregnant night
until he came for her.

The distant voices
that would not let her die
without her Rangi
to stroke her hair
as she led him back
into the fiction
they had become.

Letters We Never Sent

In Xanadu did Kubla Khan
A stately pleasure dome decree
Where Alph, the sacred river, ran
Through caverns measureless to man
Down to a sunless sea.

    –Coleridge

white sails over dark water
the Opera House keeps watch
for the next onslaught by sea
but the expatriate drifts down
by Cathay Pacific econo class

entrusting his craft to a city
that promotes an airline to prove
it's an entity with *chutzpah* [1][2]
and speaks in hard currency —
no unwashed empires need apply

he returns his seat to the upright
and surrenders his earphones
always the foot soldier at heart
the touchdown is methodical
and his lover says *we're home*

he believes this climax applies
to him a new stanza just like that
so he slips out of his hypnosis
tucking his old skin under the seat
for some indifferent attendant

to stuff into a black plastic bag
with the inevitable flotsam/litter
of yet another voyage terminating
on predictable tarmac there are
no more surprises only discos

the silence at night

to excite the stomach to hunger
and the queues of the compliant
lead from embarkation to exit
without a hint of complaint
they wouldn't have their luggage

torn for the sake of a poem
no more couplets only smalltalk
to pass the time from soap opera
to quiz show and the cola
loses its fizz so quickly these days

under the hypnosis of halftones
the blare of xanadu redigitised
the sheen of the polished floor
and the quality assured carpet
of Sydney International Airport —

home indeed

at least they speak English

well sort of

[T]hey have no tincture of barbarity, cruelty, suspicion
or revenge. They are ever of an even unruffled temper,
slow to anger and soon appeased and as they have no suspicion
so they ought not to be suspected, and an hour's acquaintance
is sufficient to repose an entire confidence in them.[13]

This god
a sort of Neptune
was asleep at the bottom of the sea
when this stupid fisherman

wandered
by and snagged his hook
in the god's hair wakening him.

Furious at this impertinence
Neptune sputtered to the surface
and decided that the innocent
should perish for this insult
and only the fisherman
would be spared.

You had to be a god
to make any sense of it.
It can't be easy to be top dog —
lights out in your salty palace —
if you were lonely who'd distil
your tears from the ocean?
Maybe he mistook the fisherman
for a kindred spirit of sorts

and spared him for his pride
which the gods usually reserve
for themselves and a few special
artists with that spark of divinity
which forces them to sleep fitfully
out of sight out of mind.

Most mortals are expendable
for the sake of one fine canvas
a perfect brushstroke that shocks
the sky so the barnacled monarch
ordered this Noah to take his family
straight onto the *toa marama*

which some Tahitians call an island
others a mountain but it's really

the silence at night

a moon warrior an ark that floats
above the sooty clouds of the mediocre
so the earth can have another chance
to mimic the wings of inspiration

until society gets back on its feet again
the designer gowns the delicious parfumé
fleshy diversions the dove left to flap
against the wind the artist to deflate
in some corner bleeding unscented wax
while Neptune groans at the punch line.

give me that old time religion

he'd given his children a taste
of what it meant to be Jewish
clinging to debris at the whim

of whitecaps where every cruise ship
brandishes a crucifix in the face
of the storm and parenthesises you

of course they were too innocent
to hate or to know why the flesh
of the pig and the lobster was a sin

but then he'd never been a proper Jew
let his sideburns bristle or worn
a skullcap or chanted with the old men

on *shabat* with sunlight slanting
through stained glass onto a Torah
so who was *he* to fiddle on a flimsy roof?

Of course their mother won them over
he decided to write to/for them instead
of leaving breadcrumbs for them to follow

from bookshop to bookshop
or even library to library *hallelujah*
while he kept ahead of the shattered

glass the virtual bombs of jealousy
trying to mesmerise the brokers of power
with splinters of bone and gold fillings

and undertakings never to outshine
the efforts of their plodding offspring
who could not see God in a porpoise

give me that old time religion

or philosophy in a lump of coral
how he'd ducked out of focus before
their anthologies had detected him

improvising the promised land
imagining Sinai by night in words
of shivering clay an inflatable ghetto

that holograms the burning bush
in his mind into an old time religion
that keeps roaring back no matter

which network you switch to
but he still knows the hymns off
by heart and that's what betrays him

lets their crowbars jimmy his attic
in Chicago or Warsaw or London
and you can't depend on your mates

when the chips are down it's every
poet for himself on this imploding
planet of art so you chant out loud

*our God and God of our fathers
may Thy blessing rest upon us
according to the gracious promise*

of Thy word and the opera house
is appeased grants you a subscription
leeward from the homogeneity

of skinheads and other zealots
of the monochrome page *Hear o Israel
the Lord our God the Lord is One*

Letters We Never Sent

The first Maori and first European —
one digs up taro or pulls an oar
in the hot sun while the other dozes
all day in the shade — why is that?

Here is their story:

you see God made two men
one brown one white and he couldn't
make up his mind which one to bless
so he decided just to watch them a while

well brown man he was happy just
to sing and dance and wear flowers
in his hair so God gave him an island
with a lagoon and lots of fish to spear

then brown man was no trouble at all
but white man was always muttering
don't want this and don't want that
and he couldn't sing a note or dance

and God said 'I didn't do very well
with *this* one' so he made up his mind
to give white man something to really
complain about so he set him down

on an island where the soil was bad
and the sea was freezing and the fish
were clever and quick and God left
those men like that for a while but after

a thousand years or so he came back
thinking maybe he'd been too hard
on white man so he lowered two boxes
from heaven and gave the first choice

give me that old time religion

to brown man who being greedy like all Maoris
rushed over and snatched the big one
leaving white man with the smaller box
still grumbling and whining the whole time

brown man found a shovel and axe in his
while white man found pen paper and ink
and God said they had to work with those
forever — bad mistake we made that day!

Be not afeard, the isle is full of noises,
Sounds, and sweet airs, that give delight and hurt not.
Sometimes a thousand twangling instruments
Will hum about mine ears; and sometimes voices
That if I then had wak'd after long sleep
Will make me sleep again, and then in dreaming,
The clouds methought would open, and show riches
Ready to drop upon me, that when I wak'd
I cried to dream again.

    — *The Tempest*

If only I could paint this!

The man who was to become a new chief
emerged from his house in rich garments
the most important people of the island
crowded in close but didn't dare
touch him for fear

of the high ariois [14]
who led the way to the *marae*
their heads decked with the rarest
of feathers. Such a wash of brilliant
colour beneath the heavy clouds!

Then the priests gave the signal
with a burst of trumpets and drums
and withdrew into the temple
from which a dead man a sacrifice
was set down before the icon

of the gods
and the chief and the priests began
their cries and chants to heaven
after which the high priest lent over
the victim and tore out his eyes

the right one he set before the icon
the left one he offered to the king
who opened his mouth as if
to swallow it but the priest
snatched it back restoring it

to the corpse.
The lesser priests bore the idol
down to the shore on a carved bier
followed by the chief who sat stiffly
on the shoulders of the other chiefs

with the trumpets and drums again
and the priests prancing in the sand
and the people eager for a miracle.
When they reached the sacred canoe
they gently lowered the icon into it.

After they stripped the chief naked
the high priest led him into the sea
so the *Atouas-mao* [15] could caress
and wash him and then he returned
to the canoe where he was wrapped

give me that old time religion

with a *Maro-ourou* about his loins
and a *Taoumata* around his head
as signs of sovereignty for the people
who broke their silence with cries
of *Maeva Arii!* [16] from every side.

And so they returned to the *marae*
where the chief was set down again
before the icon to await a wave of
naked men and women who covered him
in a dance of urine and excrement

which perhaps they did to remind him
how petty we mortals are in the sight
of a god even those who are crowned
rise and fall in the breath of a dream.

(misguided artists
pathetic kings)

the internet

do you remember Pennsylvania Avenue
before the barricades before
the insults were fired point blank
at the White House
at no particular President
Lyndon Lyndon
how many men have you
killed today

back then democracy was still
within reach and our leaders
worked a crowd without fear

shaking hands with real people
instead of poseurs who ham it up
wrapped in stars and stripes

under interrogation
the accused insisted the machine-
gun had a purpose of its own —
'I was just an agent of voices
who came to me in a blinding
light and said thou shalt do
all that we command'

and of course the bullets
spoke in an intricate hypertext
back to the eternal flame
a blade of truth beyond the woods
of uncertainty which was why
he asked to be left in solitary
so the connection would not
be severed

it was 'with the profoundest
regret' that the President signed
the order to transform the street
into a 'safety zone' of potted
trees and flowers no mention
of bunkers

sometimes at dawn he strolls
in the roof garden of missiles
to rehearse his scripts
pausing on impulse
to knight a sentry
with a sword of cliches

<HTML>

give me that old time religion

In a dark time, the eye begins to see,
I meet my shadow in the deepening shade;
I hear my echo in the echoing wood...

    –Theodore Roethke

he comes out of his cocoon
just for the talkshow
wary of dark replays

Salman Rushdie superstar
a centrefold of thoughtful
makeup and judicious

lighting he arches
then dries his wings
as if he has all the time

in the world and no one dares
to challenge his doctrine
he speaks to a steady red eye

anticipates the instant when
it will leap from one camera
to the next 'life's a pretext

then you're forced to recant'
what's important is to keep
your focus on the substance

and not let the ocean dislodge
you with its fuming undertow
Allah is great Allah is mighty

the raven sits on your shoulder
pecks at your ear drawing a drop
of blood as you scribble out a fresh

chapter *Allah is the only truth*
who can be secure when fictions
are strip searched for infidelity

forget about your novitiates
the politically correct clerics
have gained the high ground

and the writing workshops
so you'll have to stay after school
and clap the erasers for Allah

or compose letters to yourself
in cryptics no critics can decode
Allah's dust is sweet on the tongue

<HTML>

if you read the small print for this software
you'll find no protection against designer
viruses the *eboli* that infiltrate fibre-optic
DNA *the purchaser hereby warrants*

*the dealer free of malpractice by opening
this seal* is it curiosity that compels you
or a thirst for scripts? the risk is what
it's all about — keeping boredom at bay

your hand trembles on the mouse
press ENTER *to begin* you're told
there are so many menus to browse
so many choices panting against lamp-

posts offering you the spill of your life
but you still go for the e-mail

give me that old time religion

and key in her number by heart
waiting until your modems dock

```
are you there, Italy? you ask
wide awake she replies come sta?
thanks for the photo — you're lovely
but nothing more than you deserve

il dolce well I feel I can tell you
anything in spite of the distance —
or is that because you're so far away?
I can be close as you like, Australia

at your fingertips or in your head
what more could you want?  I want
to be in bed with you—there
I've said it then there's a pause
```

and you freeze as the cursor pulses
perhaps you've gone too far perhaps
you should have stayed with the drought
or the starving topics of Rwanda

so she'd believe you were a man with
higher values *mi dispiace* 17 she says
```
you caught me off guard there —
you want that we talk dirty now?
```

this might be a trap, you think
a pit along the path of gender wars
```
I'd like to meet your family, Italy
but you're Jewish — and that

would make things very hard with papa
I'm more lonely than Jewish you say
```

31

and almost mean it but then there's
nothing and even the cursor dissolves

finally this scrawl appears
YOUR CONNECTION HAS BEEN SEVERED
COURTESY OF JEW-BUSTER SQUAD # 2
CONVERT OR BE DAMNED!

you go to bed shivering
have to wank to get to sleep
tomorrow you'll change attics
and renounce the internet

```
arrivederci, Italy!
```

</HTML>

intoxicants

Here is the pit for our land
the grave for it
that is the foreign spirits.

It is the pit which causes
all the sorrow
to the mothers and children.

    —Queen Makea of Avarua

making Manihiki beer:

bake a half dozen coconuts
of the sweeter tasting variety
in an earth oven until soft

remove and open them
cutting out the white meat
and softening it more
by beating gently
with a pounder

place the meat in a strong
cloth and compress by twisting
until all the juice is extracted
then break the husk into small
pieces and twist in the cloth
in the same way

let the juice from the husks flow
into the juice from the kernels
and then into plastic, stainless
steel or glass (never a tin)

carefully cover and set aside
to ferment

in a couple of days
you'll have a fine drop
of sweet and potent beer
and the world as your friend

on the boardwalk from the Opera House
she cradles her cask
shades it from sun

she's teaching it to read
her lips *black fellas should be
seen but never heard*

then she hears singing
from under the sails
(it's Dame Kiri in *La Traviota*

an exception who unsettles
the rule with hardly any makeup
the colour's already there)

Johnno has wet his pants
again she can see a dull dark
patch by the zip spreading

gradually down his thighs
as he squats down next to her
squinting at the cask

'the loo' she says 'didn't you---'
'I made there in time' he slurs
'but I had to wait while this kid

intoxicants

finished his ice cream before
he shook his dick and moved
out of me way but by then I'd

lost it and him staring at me
as if he'd seen a ghost
'the singing' she says

'I heard it while you was pissing
how come I only hear music
when you is away?'

'give me a taste of that cask'
he says 'and I'll tell you
it's easier when my lips
are wet' so she takes him
in her lap where the salt breeze
can blow across his jeans

and as she opens the tap
to suckle him she wonders
what it would be like to sink

in the posh seats just once
before she passes on to hear
the singing the notes soaring

so high above the crags
that the seabirds go dizzy
trying to catch the updraught

to high E and beyond
and for a fraction she feels
something in her throat

a vibrato pushing up
through the blues and greens
of anaemic chords gasping

for air but she drops it
as she feels the nightstick
jab in her ribs — 'push on!'

    * * *

it could be in Hobart or Christchurch
this tidy fish and chips shop in Raro
except there they wouldn't serve
mahi-mahi though they might have
Bunny behind the counter sternly
shaking the chips

she knows we won't be back
so what's the point of pretending
she enjoys her work?

the fillet is enormous
and the chips thick but crisp
and she grunts in the direction
of the tomato sauce and vinegar
as she takes our money
and passes back the change

an old friend comes in
he's been fishing the outer islands
but now he's come back to the big
smoke for a shave they talk about
kids and how boring it is for them
'they fish all day and drink all night'
says Bunny whose two boys are in
Auckland now waiting on the dole

intoxicants

he says he'll take her somewhere
exotic when he wins the lottery
which he's certain will be quite soon
'problem is I forgot to put in a ticket
this year' he says 'maybe next time then'

she doesn't smile even at that
and when we thank her for the food
she seems surprised at the gesture
after all what's the point in giving thanks
when you've already paid?

and I remember her with this
even though she forgot us before
we were out the door.

the natives slip over the dust
in bare feet the waving draperies
of the long gowns of the women

add to the undulating movement
which carries them along

    –John La Farge [18]

He was wrong to try to crack
the sweet meat of their silence.

A string of words may be a lie
but the breath between them
will spawn a prism if you wait

so take a sip of nightair
from your agenda of secrets
and close your eyes to contours.
Inspiration's an eccentric moon —

if you try to adjust the lens
try to urge it into the familiar
the colour will flap away into
grey anthems everyone hums
but no one bothers to sing.
That's why I prefer those moments
of stubborn rock before sunrise
when I face the syncopations
of a cliff-face with my fingers

before daylight gives it purpose
before the sea and its backdrop
remind me of the perspectives
and the purpose that I fled.

For fame?
Or out of fear of gravity?

It is responsibility
that shackles us
makes us drunk with families
confusing/diffusing our energy
in the mud of priorities.

You cannot be consummate
head of house *and* artist.
You must itch for excellence
for there'll be demons in the grass
if you entertain a compromise.

So you drain the glass
and choose what's already
chosen a slab of uncertainty
where society fades in and out
and you sketch your nightmares

intoxicants

all in all
a European can do well
on an atoll
and much more safely
than in a city provided
he knows how to fish
uses mercurochrome on his cuts
carefully scours his cooking pans
with sand and water and takes care
to get his chores finished
before darkness sets in

mosquitoes are kept at bay
with dry pieces of palm bark
which smoulder with an unforgettable
aroma the whole night long

then you can light a pipe and listen
to the call of a migrating bird
the whispering of fronds in the breeze
the ceaseless rumbling of the reef
the soft indefinable sound of the atoll
a crooning child in sleep

and you know this is
home

the internet

someone decided to torch the French
consulate in Perth last night

the voice on the phone muttered
something about 'liberation'

and the 'Pacific Front'
the usual claptrap of striking
a blow against complicity

I could tell it was a mobile phone
her voice fading during the angry bits
growing stronger as she strung out
the cliches 'kill the bastards kill...'

by the time we made it to the scene
the firemen were already there
and the fireball was nearly spent
then the honorary consul rolled up
and I had to tell him the score
before the cameras hooked him

he was rather soft spoken
for a plastic surgeon
who dispensed a drizzle of visas
between facial reconstructions
hadn't been back to France for ages
didn't see why the sky had decided
to fall in on him

it did seem rather silly
grumpy men playing with bombs
if you've got one you've got
to pull it out otherwise what's
the point of having one, right?

the pollies checked the marketshare
then declared the plan unAustralian
an barbarous act of terror
even as they smashed innocent
bottles of French champagne

and swore off berets for at least
a week 'our children are too
precious' and blah blah...
I reckon the monarchists
missed their chance —
you wouldn't catch old Liz
shitting in someone else's nest
even if the dump's out of sight
and nearly out of mind

too long for a Letter to the Editor
and too concise for a novel —
any ideas out there?

<HTML>

Space-filled, reflecting the seasons, the folk-lore
Of each of the senses; call it, again and again,
The river that flows nowhere, like a sea.

    —Wallace Stevens

the creek before sunrise —
a lisp of fog slightly grey
from early fumes

worries the grass with frost
a freeway rising in your ears
stresses at deadlines splayed

across your memory banks
that detach the stanzas between
appointments with limp head-

lights but the creek persists
becomes a nagging mirror
for the dark phalanx of trees

jerking the sky out of focus
muting any promise of pink —
a shock of rain on Sunday

swept the clinging rabble away
so the snag has no spectators
to threaten with a chilly sermon

there must be more to graffiti
than waiting knee-deep in muck
for an angel to strike up the band

just so the ambitious can ferry
across in four-part harmony
to a place where movies are free

then flying fish shatter the mirror
the daydream bristles at its cue
and you press the accelerator again

<HTML>

Bring him down—bring him down!
Low and inconspicuous! I'd not have him ride
on the wagon at all — damn him —
the undertaker's understrapper!

      –William Carlos Williams

not easy to be born of fame
poor Charles van Doren
son of Mark brother of Amy
and so on down the tree

they were all brilliant really
ivy league from heel to crown
and everything they touched

turned at least to pewter
if not anthology

it was never a question
of when but where and how
much the winning would be
Columbia needed him far more
than he needed a university
and his students worshipped
his aurora especially the girls
who dreamt of undressing
for his scrupulous lectern
he could have encamped
under any of their cots

going on *21* [19] must have been
the adolescence he missed
a climb to the narrowest rung
where flirting with balance
really was an issue
he might have been James Dean
or John Lennon or even
Nelson Mandela daring bullets
but always keeping the adulation
fixed squarely between his eyes

seeing how high he could soar
until his feathers began to melt
between the furious commercials
for the free-fall to confession
before a congregation of millions
though he'd have suffered any
pain to have spared his father
the shock that his couplets
had spilt into a waste land

to seize to seize I know
that dream

<HTML>

shedding skin

dear Mette

I have sent eight canvases to France.
Naturally many will be incomprehensible
and so let me explain the hardest
which is really the one I'd prefer to keep
Manao Tupapaü [20] — nude of a young girl —
unless you can sell it for a very good price.

There will be those who say her pose
is indecent who can think only of coquettes
caught in a garden at twilight mischief
but you must point to her expression
which captures the very real dread
Maoris have of spirits.

The colours are meant to ring sadly
like a funeral bell — purple dark blue
orangey yellow. And then her linen
(made from beaten tree bark) a greenish
yellow to suggest the reassuring light
Kanakas must have before they dare

to sleep. Show them how my yellow
links the orangey tints to the blue
to make a soft chord without a hint
of lamplight and the flowers — oh yes
they are to be phosphorescences of night
the souls of the dead so I make them

mere glimmers in the background
to conjure the shadow she imagines
the double of herself without flesh

shedding skin

that we *all* must confront at the end.
Spoon it to the critics like that, my pet
and they'll think you most scholarly!

We leave lovers behind then meet
others who are just as discontented

with who they are and where
they are as the ones we left

behind and it's all an endless
loop the unzipping the stepping

out and shredding of skin
in episodes behind failsafe doors

where we shadow-play with strangers
and do the things that make foreplay

almost exciting until the retake
reminds us of the track we thought

we'd left behind but if we replay
our lines in a new context is that

a lie or an impulse to better
our past mistakes? And if we talk

at all of purpose in this altercation
in this naked rebuttal of future

we'll see the present object recoil
into an icon of the female principle

the pleading eyes the pouting mouth
that teases us to acknowledge *her*

if not her role before your words
strike the bedrock of the familiar

the charred meat chef would like
to uncook. So you let her stroke you

into orgasm as if it's the sticky stuff
that really matters and at the peak

it is
ah it *is*

déjà-vu

Encore qu'en comparant attentivement
dans l'une on peut lire
je tombe
et dans l'autre
tu tombes.
Qui tombe?
Toi le lecteur,
ou moi le gribouilleur?
Tout dépend dans quelle mémoire
nous sommes.

    —Philippe Genty

Am I really getting younger
or do I keep tripping over
memories of things
yet to be?

It used to be so linear:
on your mark get set go
quick-stepping rocks across
a rising creek no fear
of free-fall you were the stellar
glint of everything your parents
had mortgaged with dreams
and once the entry was bought
there could be no turning back
no apology to nausea
as you entered the terminal
and let the electric footpath
ease you to the predestined
gate onto a seat where you'd be
plucked by a woman who smiled

and spoke of your future as if
it was past and all you had to do
was let the pathetic present
catch up

in the dark between time-zones
she slipped off your clothes and rubbed
your face your neck your shoulders
with scent but the climax would have
to wait for a proper denouement
meanwhile she'd give up Europe for you
what was travelling anyway but a trick
to distract us from the classifieds
of life? you'd heard the pitch before
but there was no time to remaster
the tape and fudge the credits
while you queued on the tarmac
and you could feel the cabin shudder
as the brakes fought the engine's thrust
until it was full throttle into turbulence
and suddenly you were through it
into the sedated air of a contract in blood
balanced/responsible/dependable
you reclined the seat and tuned in Bach
as you watched her take off her clothes
and cheered on by the business class
mount you ready set go

so this was marriage
so this is what the past meant
when it bad-mouthed the future
with cartoons and now you open
your eyes and see yourself
hurtling past the window
falling through clouds
into a candy-spun present

déjà-vu

without a parachute
did you forget your star-sign?
or did you remember it
and decide to jump anyway?

never mind
she's captured your sperm
but the ultimate thrill
lies ahead ready set

  * * *

A Mixed Bag At Breakfast — Edgewater Resort

Cyril just retired from a desk job
had no idea food could be so time-consuming
as he scans his encore of ripe mangoes
and lets his wife rattle on
about the frightful choice of tours
her breasts used to be tropical
but now everything about her person
is stretched and mean
oh but the sunshine — isn't it grand?

two twin sisters from Dublin
inseparable since their husbands died
only months apart from 'congestion
of the liver' or so the doctors said
to be more tactful than cirrhosis
nick a few muffins and pats of butter
for morning tea won't be noticed
regally munched on their balcony

the anarchist professor
tastes the air like a monitor

eyes darting through the conference schedule
for premmie theories easiest prey
wiping all trace of yolk from his plate
with triangles of enriched white bread
he hums Palestrina in perfect pitch

and Mr Useless (his tag not mine)
who flirts with you about bushwalks
to muddy caves then wants you to put in
two dollars for the crab race at lunchtime
'I know a sure thing when I seize it'
(his words not mine) before I come back
with our coffees and he slinks away
for a better chance of woman

Polynesian Night

Cyril has changed
Cyril has caught his breath
Cyril is florescent orange shorts
and a purple top and purple socks
with brown sandals which his wife
bought for him one Boxing Day
at Dover and Cyril tried to kiss her lips
but had to settle for a fleeting cheek
(she knew where such manners might lead)
now Cyril breathing hotly on his Pentax
to capture the unsanctioned thrill
of womanflesh (a leer at the primitive
can be disavowed without a wafer)

the Dublin twins did without lunch
to afford this so it better be bloody good!
they order a carafe of chianti and crusty

déjà-vu

buns when the grass skirts come on
goggle at the imperative masculinity
pounding the dance floor
oh yes it's all coming back oh
yes yes yes or my name's not
Molly Bloom

the anarchist professor returned unscathed
from question time to wade into the surf
barefoot despite the warnings of stonefish
leaps high buildings with a single bound
and dines on raw fish with gin and bitter lemon
chasers as his reward then stares at the dancers
thanking his lucky stars he wasn't born a savage
aber eine ubermensch — naturlich!

Mr Useless was nowhere to be seen
he'd lost his shirt in the crab compo
to a pair of grannies from Auckland
who took him for double-or-nothing
at poker over date scones and tea —
otherwise I rather enjoyed the performance
until the blasted battery in my video ran dry

to Aline 21

You would have me better
than I can ever be —
father, and perfect friend
a flame on which to temper

the sword of your sketches
a lagoon of experience
opaque and salty in its depth

Letters We Never Sent

yet sentient.
You plunge in
holding your breath as long
as you can and even longer
down and down and down

to that gallery of coral
where lungs are forgotten
to find the pearls that are
my signature.

You understand the savage
in me and in yourself.
You demand no apologies
from those sirens of colour

who drew your father away
to a channel he must navigate
to shape faces from shadows
and give utterance to fog.

Even so Mademoiselle must be off
to her ball where she'll dazzle
the young men with her dancing
and they'll try to court her

by swearing that my paintings
somehow *speak* to them.
I'll always remember that night
in Copenhagen when you said

'later on I'll be your wife'.
Your eyes were clear and calm
in the lamplight and I wanted
to dedicate some words to those

déjà-vu

moments of innocence before
I set sail again leaving you bare
to the wind. But I had to bury you
so far away with useless tears

the only flowers for your tomb
before I could fill this notebook.
Can you read it? Can you hear me
swear I no longer embrace God!

They dismissed it as a tropical slum
Aitutaki the emerald island
they who have no respect for history
whispered from father to son
who can not tolerate the pristine
without a cross on the highest peak

yet the warriors then were hardy
with their *teka* 22   that would bounce
against the rocks and pierce a foe
from his blind side

until the whalers came.

What their bullets spared
the missionaries' bibles subdued
but their sermons were laced
with measles and even those
who refused the baptism
felt their knees liquefy

and then the Marines came.

They left religion and mortgages
at the dock with their wives.

53

Letters We Never Sent

After all this was war this was
hell and it's so hard to inspire
menfolk who've never heard
of Gary Cooper or John Wayne
without smearing a bit of mud
on your face without priming
their women with whisky

and then the Marines moved on.

They still show cowboy flicks
from time to time lest they forget
but when a man paddles to shore
against a crimson sky with his prow
heavy with fish he may see ghosts
as he stumbles the lonely *bohir* [23]
a naked girl with glowing lipstick
a man with an ironwood spear
trying to bluff away the devils
who struck down his daughter
with measles

but at dawn there's nothing more
than a tatty poster from Hollywood
and a rusty drum filled with empty
bottles of spirits and beer cans

until the tourists were shanghaied.

the internet

Six days was long enough.
They did their job.

> −Bill Clinton

déjà-vu

famous as the Kentucky Colonel
for a week or so
pilot Scott O'Grady
rescued by Warthogs and Harriers
(or his faith in God?)
from behind "enemy" lines

who knows where your friends
cease and the enemy fire begins?
in the shifty mountains of Bosnia
it's no wonder radar gets confused
there are too many prayers cluttering
the airwaves too many gods jamming

the signal as tracers flare the nightsky
locking onto Satan and his trainees
parachuting into the molten truces
at least with Sadam
we knew where we stood
not this bog between Coke and Pepsi

but the kids back home still need heroes
and the President's men are running short
of excuses and the cereal ads are apathetic
something went wrong in Mudville
after cholesterol struck out the Babe
and Elvis began to believe his lyrics
and Muhammud couldn't remember his

now
after all the fuss is over
Scotty stands tall and tells them
'I'm not a hero' which means
'I didn't go down with my plane'
but the ghost writers are a-scribblin'

and the agents are anticipatin'
the rights for the film and rock CD
there's not a opportunity to lose
in Bosnia the footage is still rolling
and corpses are free for the asking
and there's always a fresh pilot
on thaw in the wings

<HTML>

There was a bang after all.
The earth had had enough
of diplomacy and dithering.

how much concrete and steel
does it take to break
a planet's patience?

We were asleep on our futons
when the letter burst its seal.
The walls turned to chalk dust
as I reached for you but then
the timber beams came down
and you were crushed.

they said Tokyo would be first
to explode, these people of fact
that we worship

I stood there in the gusts
of burning flesh, winter sky
pouring down through the gap
then I dropped to my knees
and cried out for another beam.
Why should *I* be left behind?

déjà-vu

*that freeway over there —
they swore it would last
longer than our emperor*

Inside is death: outside, rescue.
A woman teeters on the shattered
bricks of her house. She wears
a fine leather coat from Italy.
She will sleep in it tonight
after she banishes the police.

*at dusk children sift ashes
slowly through their fingers
to find their father's bones*

<HTML>

good news
for a change

though a bit hard
for those who take their dose
at meal times but here goes
nothing, listeners:

Louise Robinson, 13,
of Winona Falls, Washington
this morning received a new
ear but not just *any* ear
and not really an ear at all
but a piece of cartilage
grown in her arm for months
then a trim and tuck and
presto: an ear-to-be.

ugh!
how she lost it in the first place
my sources don't say

use your poetic license
or whatever you journos call
imagination these days

only don't make it a knife —
the moms and pops will know
that quacks can make quick work
of mishaps like that with needles
though how the blood decides
to trickle through and when
is enough of a miracle for most
churchgoers

make it a fire
an electric blanket gone feral
something like that
something irreversible
bad luck
maybe an act of God
Lloyd's of London turf
something like that

Van Gogh?
no this isn't a bleeding arts
program and there's nothing
about her passion to paint
or even write though she *might*
take up sculpting one day
if her mother lets her out
since she likes a slap of wet clay

déjà-vu

no keep it simple stupid:
your camera at a respectful
distance from the scar tissue
a slight blur or even a shadow
will heighten their suspense —
to grow or not to grow
that is the question

'and what about earrings, Louise?'

(she giggles, blushes)
'the surgeon thinks they'll be OK
but I haven't picked them out yet.'

how's that, Vince?

cut!

</HTML>

settling in

to Paul Sérusier

When you are far from your land
and quite alone in the country
letters give you much pleasure —
so you must write to me often
my dear Sérusier.

I cannot tell if what I'm doing
is good I cannot get outside
myself to see if this is substance
or madness I paint so furiously
and yet there's nothing there.

If only you were here.
If only *anyone* were here
who could speak of art
or even in proper French.
Why must I be all or nothing

for my work? Yes, some day
I'll return with enough sketches
to guarantee a salary of canvases
so I can afford to live to paint
rather than the other way around.

Sometimes I find their language
eludes me. I cannot memorise
cannot concentrate on anything
but this cascade of dreams
and yet they look after me

as if I was their child
bringing me fish and coconuts
asking for nothing in return
except to know that I'm content
in heart. And we call *them* savages?

I must penetrate their being
and walk among their gods
to understand this generosity —
perhaps *they* are the continent
and we the castaway island

or maybe this is just infatuation
that will diminish once I reach
the bare sinew of this race.
But I am determined to be richer
for this deprivation and sharpen

my eye for the flower of simplicity.
So back to work but remember me
to Filiger for the idea of this music
and mandolin. With all this practice
I must be more of a virtuoso than he!

The city of home is empty of people.
All its songs are the songs of exile.

    —Tom Shapcott

dear J.

do you remember the last time
I came back?

you were in the yard as I drove up
and you pretended to be invisible
afternoon shadow between trees
dropping low to the ground

then gone

never really my flesh
though you wanted to be
eclipsed/cooling moon
left to rise among sisters
rigid windows trapped air

the tug of family bickering
with each vertical you bashed
letters meant but never sent
for/to me

did I ever tell you I read you
clearly despite the distance
despite the static we put
between us?

perhaps
it was better that you have
two objects for pure hatred
the father you never knew
before the father you knew
and lost

brutal ghosts for diaries
half Slavey [24] half Quebecois
tribes of Abraham wandering
somewhere between snow
and the muddy green of thaw

the sea saw it and fled
the Jordan turned backwards

what does it mean to adopt
a child? as if we can configure
our blood to spurt from dry rock
into a miracle that invigorates
the grey skin of marriage

at the presence of the God of Jacob
who turned the flint into a fountain

to be a father
to be a proper father
is to know the conjugation
yet not insist that your son
wear it as his birthright

I feel better for that
I feel better
I feel

do you?

It was hard to relax on Mangaia.

I came ashore on the crest of a wave
with five men sweating at their oars
hissing between their teeth.

No one spoke of the girl who got seasick
and was swept away in the storm.
It was her tough luck not theirs.

The Mangaians watch each other
very closely for signs of treachery
except in church where the pews
face away from each other

and the factions slap out hymns
as though the weakest will be cut
from the herd and sacrificed
to appease some imported god.

I want to seal my roof with pandanus
fronds because they last longer
but only *kavana* 25 are permitted.
Such arrogance!

It's a matter of blood
not price and I have to wield
a sickle by order of the governor
when my gardener Noo forgets
to trim the weeds.
Yet they will trust me
to sew up a neighbour's leg
slashed by a pig just before
it was butchered. He doesn't
flinch under my darning needle

and promises not to tell anyone
of this otherwise every accident
will come to me and sooner
or later something will go wrong
which will be *my* tough luck.

It was hard to relax on Mangaia
yet I managed it until my coconut
leaf roof began to leak — why?

masks

The sea was not a mask. No more was she.
The song and water were not medleyed sound.
Even if what she sang was what she heard,
Since what she sang was uttered word by word.

    –Wallace Stevens

dear M.

a mask can be an excuse
for not writing

it seals in anger
until thought becomes
a curse and curse becomes
jagged tin embedded in sand
before the salt hardens it
into rust

submerged is safer
from the talons of air
there's a ruthless certainty
in the currents you carry —
the liquefaction of your mind

why do we yearn for land anyway?
solids are the exception
not the rule

as you paddle among the coral
it grants you naming rights
and you try to define the fish
by colour ignoring the spines

you would stay here forever
if your words weren't so pale
then the mask springs a leak

the sea roars in your eyes
as you surface to realise
you've been straddling
the seismic all along

it's back to square one
as lava stalemates into rock
as your anger disperses among
the tidepools and the mobs
of disillusioned shells

you clear your lungs
and scratch my name
in the sand with a damp stick
father
three years is a long time

Sam Hardcase and Larry Cypress
were two traders unlike as friends
could be. Sam took a Maori to marry

and kept his sense of humour for it
while Larry stayed celibate and moody.
He'd write one day he swore or paint or

do *something* special if only
he could stop drinking long enough
to direct his genius.

As the years went on Sam grew fat
on his wife's charms but Larry became
lean as well as celibate and moody.

masks

He wrote a few ballads about pirates
then gave up on words, painted Still Life
With Coconuts but that was *too* still

finally glued bits of coral and shell
into "expressions" which he left
on the beach to dare the tide

then draped them with seaweed
or whatever chance left tangled
at their feet. It was a good idea

and Sam bought one for his yard
but the other people were scared
evil spirits might be hiding in them.

Larry went on a binge one night
smashed his bleached gallery
then took too many sleeping pills.

Sam found him half-dead
in a pool near the reef.
He dragged him into shore

and gave him mouth-to-mouth
but poor Larry was cold and flaccid
until Sam slipped him a little strychnine

on a kill-or-cure. The poor blighter
went stiff as his Still Life for a minute
then his face flushed lobster-red

and burst into a tremendous sweat.
Soon after he sat bolt upright in bed
and let out a scream that would have

popped out the nails in a coffin
before sagging back on his pillow
eyes wide open and mumbling

while Sam gave him warm milk
for the rest of the night. He made it
but gave up on art after that.

How lucky you are to be in Paris!
That is where the top people are
and you should certainly consult
a specialist who could cure your
madness. Are we all not mad?

    –Van Gogh to Gauguin

to Mette

I have worked through it now
I know this soil and no longer
have to smear it on my lips
to taste the scent of clay.

I have reached that plateau
where my feet can be in France
while my senses are in Oceania.
I can *reside* among the Maoris
with no need for translation
or fumbling for masks

and I am confident
that no one back home
is doing what I am doing now.
I have made — no
Tahiti has remade *me*

masks

and that will breathe
a difference into my art

though what it *is* I cannot say
for if I try to describe it precisely
I would surely do it an injustice.
The more I dwell on boundaries
the more ill defined I become.

Other artists? I *suppose* I miss them
the exceptional ones who paint
no matter what the risk might be.
Like poor Vincent [26] who still
haunts me whenever I think
of sunflowers and harsh light.

I am too conspicuously in control —
that's why the others blame me
for his death but am I less an artist
for not lashing my breast
until my blood finds a course
that can be sold as inspiration
to make a rich man richer?

If you could have seen him, Mette
that snowy morning on the Rue Lepic
bundled in a goatskin like a drover
a bristling fur hat (of rabbit no doubt)
bristling red beard *everything* bristling
except those blue eyes so clear so keen
too intelligent to be a vagabond's

watch him slip into a dealer's shop
rubbing some warmth into his hands
among those primitive arrows

tarnished rings and cheap paintings
under his arm a small still life
a pink crayfish on pink paper —
he wants to sell it to pay his rent.

The dealer recognises him in a flash
'ah my friend' he sighs 'the customers
only ask for grubby Millets and besides
the Renaissance is on the Boulevard
and your crayfish looks a bit unhappy
but they say you have some talent
so I'd like to do a favour for you
here take a hundred sous!' [27]

The coin spins on the counter
and Vincent plucks it with thanks
and trudges back up the Rue Lepic
and is nearly safely at his lodgings
when a woman fresh from prison
winks at him desiring his custom.

She makes him think of *La Fille Elisa* [28]
so he gives her the coin then flees
lest such irrational charity be witnessed
his stomach churning with hunger
hiding in his room from the knocking
yes the *unrelenting* knocking
that has no interest in aesthetics

and no patience for painters
especially mad ones with no respect
for honest commerce or deadlines.
When you come to throw them out
their pleas are hollow as the next man's
and their faces are temporary as winter
once spring is teasing at the door.

masks

Vincent wrote to me from the asylum
to *me* and not to them who accuse me:
all of us are insane he said
we who give ourselves up to art
despite the best advice of those
who lecture on the dangers of genius.

For him the spark lay at the lip
of some dank and twisted mineshaft
where he'd stumble in the maze
until the coal dust brought him
coughing to his knees clawing
at his eyes but then to paint

he must have thought that we
might make it to the sunlight
spill out into unpolluted air
where he might harness the voices
pounding in his skull *follow us
do not lose the scent*

So I went to Arles
to see if he could learn
to channel that fever
through his fingers.
I swear I did it for him
not myself.

*je suis sain d'Esprit
je suis Saint-Esprit* [29]

You wrote it on the purple wall
with your yellowiest brush.
Yes yellow you adored it —
you were in such a rapture
that I had come to you at last.

The Atelier du Midi [30] —
I was hardly inside the door
when you proclaimed its birth.
I was to be its proud Tartarin
wearing white linen trousers
a fat cummerbund and a bright red fez
prowling the town with my bowie knife
and knuckle dusters stalking lions
all of this expressed in bursts of flame
and sunlight flooding the Camargue
chrome yellows brilliant yellows
your poor farmhouse could hardly
contain all these grand episodes!

You showed me to my room
where sunflowers with purple eyes
stiffened against a yellow backdrop
sentries to my every movement
their stalks bathing in a yellow pot
on a yellow table as the tamer sun
streamed through the yellow curtains
to temper this flowering into gold.

When I woke up the next morning
in my yellow room I was certain
that our retreat would be fine
though we would quarrel again
and again over yellows and reds
you who depended on daylight to burn
off the fog that distracted your soul
while I stalked the perfect vermilion.

On one wall a purple still life —
two enormous shapeless shoes
the faithful ones that bore you

masks

a pastor from Holland to Belgium
down into the pits to dispense peace
to miners [31] from a Jesus who loved
the simple more than the castles
of the rich — or so you thought

you were already mad back then
weren't you?

You risked the flash of fire damp
the chrome yellow that never fails
to explode when you least expect it
and you took in one of the survivors
his face terribly burned and mutilated
and mothered him because you still
believed in miracles in your madness
and you sat with him for forty nights
keeping the air from his wounds
beating off the darkness with yellow
hymns until your miner bore a halo
and a pulsing crown of thorns
red scars on an ashen yellow forehead

beyond the shadow of a doubt
you were a madman even then.

Only Théo [32] bothered to intervene
after you were expelled from the colliery
and your family voted to bunker you
in an asylum to save you from yourself
but it only takes *one* person's faith
to persuade an artist he has it right
a beam of light against breaking tide
directing confusion into harmony
giving his visions a yellow purpose

but you were mad all the same.

I was wrong to think I could save him
I know that now — he'd write in French
and paint the wharves and boats of the Midi
in Dutch as if he were a neo-Impressionist
then leave his tubes of paint uncapped.
His finances were hopeless
and he couldn't make a soup.

He'd forget to eat for days.
'Doesn't matter' he'd say
'it's got nothing to do with discipline
you simply do the things that matter
and let the others take their turn.
A sunflower can live for weeks
without earth because then it puts
everything into its reason for being —
we live to flower not to grow!'

He'd scratch away every scab before
it healed because the sight of blood
fascinated him. 'We are fluid after all'
he'd say 'so why all this worry over
ashes? We should look to the sea.
Eternity's a wave not a worm, Paul
so raise your canvas to catch the gale!'

Then he'd try to cook a supper
like mixing colours for a landscape
and we couldn't eat it and I'd rage on
until I too forgot my pangs of hunger
and we'd collapse in a feast
of laughter then prance around
conjuring up crusts and bones.

masks

He taught me the joy of sunflowers
but I did even more for him:

I urged him back to his nature
wakened him from pale imitation
— those shackled monotonous
harmonies soft yellow on purple
purple on yellow with a gaggle
of still life in the foreground —
to the clarion call of revelation.

The speed of his progress left me
breathless as he painted a flood
of sun after sun on sun throbbing
with sun. He'd finish one scene
then spill straight into the next
as if composing a symphony
that he had to express instantly
or lose his rhythm.

One day I did a portrait of him
painting his beloved sunflowers
when I showed it to him the colour
drained from his face. 'That's me
all right' he said 'but gone mad.'

That night we went to the café
and he was content for an hour
then he ordered a light absinth
and flung it at me glass and all
his eyes ablaze.

I led him home and put him to bed
and he fell asleep in an instant.
I lay awake for ages wondering

where this madness would end.
In that grey hour just before dawn
I sensed him standing over me
but calmly. 'My dear Gauguin'
he moaned 'you must forgive me!'

'I will' I replied 'but I must go before
something worse happens and I lose
my self-control and strangle you.'
He stood there crushed in silence
then vanished as suddenly
as he'd come.

The day dragged by without a word
between us and by evening I felt
I *had* to be alone so I went for walk
along the Place Victor-Hugo
the air was heavy with the scent
of laurel and I thought it might
be all right between us after all
but then I heard a quick step
behind me and it was him
rushing at me with a razor

I should have been afraid
but I simply stood my ground
glaring until he shrank back
and ran away.

When I did not return immediately
he cut off his ear very close to his head
the blood spurting everywhere.
He flailed about on the stone floor
and staggered up the stairs to our bedroom
to staunch the flow with wet towels.

masks

But by midnight he was well enough
to pull a Basque beret over his head
and deliver the ear all washed
and wrapped to a man on duty
at a house of prostitution.
'In remembrance of me' he said
dissolving back into the night.

They found me in my hotel room
and accused me of slashing him —
my heart pounded as I rushed back
to his house and I would not wish
the dread that I felt then on anyone
I was so certain he'd killed himself
on my account.

He was curled up in bed
covered with a bloody sheet
and my fingers were trembling
as I touched his neck
but he was warm with a pulse
so I whispered to the gendarme
'kindly wake this man as carefully
as you can and if he asks for me
tell him I've departed for Paris —
the sight of me could be fatal to him.'

When the doctor finally woke him
Vincent did ask after me
but was content when they gave him
his pipe and tobacco.

They took him to the hospital
where his mind began to wander again
though he fought back to his senses

in spurts to paint his most brilliant
work in a frenzy.

His last letter came from Auvers.
He said he hoped to be well enough
to join me in Brittany though he could see
a complete cure was now out of reach.
'Dear Master' he said (the only time
he'd ever called me that) 'after knowing you
and causing you such sorrow
it's more worthy that I die in a sound
state of mind than so degraded.'

So he shot himself in the belly
and limped back to bed with his pipe
where it took him the rest of the day
to die his mind still alert with passion
for his art.

And now
when I speak of him I can say
'Vincent' gently
and mean it.

the internet

The Potato Eaters, 1885

at their evening meal
so much depends
on that dusty lamp
a kerosene halo hung
from a cross-beam

painting them as spuds
do I speak out of church?

masks

there's no patience for posing
in their expressions, Anthon [33] —
how you wronged my purpose!
this family's a wearied hand
that finds little pleasure
in forks nearly touching
over a plate of potatoes
still steaming from the oven

there's no sugar for their coffee
but the peasant who pours it
has more colour and resolve
in her downcast eyes than in any
of your precious academies —
see how her man is content
to queue for her attention?

I say we *are* what we consume —
the less a painter peels away
the more earthy the scene!

<HTML>

A Pair of Shoes, 1887

If you're to know a man's step
read the testimony of his boots

his hobnails will glint at you
through sole and scuffed heel
to testify how far he's tramped
in his sweat for satisfaction

his feet may cool for a night
but the roughshod leather

of the lolling tongue unlaced
will bear witness to the snares
he stirred up along the way

I have no choice in this
I must be a pilgrim
to forgotten tinder
even on those pathways
I have walked so many
times in unfriendly light

there will always be a fresh
branch a confluence of leaves
from an unexpected winter's
fright or an emblem of fur
clinging to a boulder that tells
of blood raging in the night

when I close my eyes the palettes
still speak the colours are waiting
for me to unchain the door
and canvass the evening's air

in the uncertain light your mind
must complete the impulse
whichever direction you choose
you come to rest on that same
shoulder of clay which demands

paint me

*or at least do
your best*

<HTML>

masks

Farmhouse in Province, 1888

I could be a cicada delighting
in the searings of daylight here
I need no shadows to temper

my hand though the others say
Monticelli [34] went quite balmy
with all these brilliant yellows

surely that's the price we pay
for these flirtations with the sun
we who come to preach of rain

in a thirsty land which others
long ago surrendered to drought
so I sketch in a peasant on his own

with blue from the sky for his shirt
and threads of gold from the grass
for his pants but when he stares off

at the farmhouse and its citadel of hay
I conjure up a wall to keep him away
and verge the wildflowers he ignored

to spite me he stumbles off the frame
for several drinks and better company
in a brash café with rough-hewn chairs

where the talk is horses and violet
thighs not the tedium of portraits
but I make a captain of him anyway

Vincent's Chair, 1888

there's something wrong
with that leg the angle perhaps
it worries about what comes
next — will the door lunge open

will my sprouting onions take fright
in the corner? alone for this long
I gain more comfort from things
than I should — the chair becomes

the artist a surface for his pipe
as the scent of tobacco fades
such a stale pouch of pretences
we make of our work, Paul [35]

well I won't be more elaborate
than my nature just to humour you
if I see a glossy floor and an empty
chair should I urge it into a clutter?

I must be careful of my nerves
to do this justice to this inspiration
this peasant backbone that bears
my weight coolly without complaint

though you ridicule it
would smash it into fuel
to fire your impatience
before you storm away

masks

Gauguin's Chair, 1888

there's no serenity in this night
yet this too is a temper of art

you have no need for morning
a flare of candle and a gaslight
are enough to make you sure
that your testament is worthy

your floor is not a solid after all
but a swatch of skittish ice-floes
clamouring for your attention
to give purpose to their pattern

but your limbs swerve away
in a practiced contempt
why should you settle for mere
promise when sirens are eager

to undress for your pleasures?
my reply is to cut off my earlobe
and deliver it delicately wrapped
to a girl at a maison de tolerance

she sponged off the scent of other
men's sex and drew me to her bed
where in the candlelight I recalled
enough of lust to bid you farewell
I think madness might be a better
friend than your lectures after all

Starry Night, 1889

why shouldn't those shining dots
in the heavens be as tangible to us
as the black splotches on a map?

just as we catch a train to reach
Tarascon or Rouen it takes death
to realise a star yet there's fibre

in those whorls of electric wind
that fingerprint the surges of God
their church is too frail to aspire

from monotony into utterance
see how that cypress mocks it
with dark flames to claim its space!

there was never such an atmosphere
in Paris where street lamps bleed
solos of bright gold from the sky

but at Saint-Rémy [36] the bars of my cell
melted away and left me speechless
before this naked fury that drew me

reeking upwards to a crescent moon
from where I could see just how flat
and insignificant our towns become

every planet has a nipple to tease us
into the sheer poetry of night and only
in orbit can we catch the speed of light

masks

Branches of an Almond Tree in Blossom, 1890

I lay on the ground for hours looking up
at this spectacle my fingers digging in

to the soft earth of spring and I suppose
someone might have thought me a corpse

as I lay there but I knew those thorns
would bear white blossoms in their season

once I got past my pain to taste the blue sky
of your joy [37] it was perhaps my best canvas

the most patiently worked thing I had done
painted with a greater dedication of touch

to show how potent fragrances can issue
from twisted branches that keep the faith

before the next day when I buckled again
like a brute—you namesaked him for me

and I can think of no greater signature
that an artist can leave than a gift of spirit

passed into unscarred hands so that when
those tender petals finally scatter to the soil

there will be nothing random in their fall
knowing the spurt of green that will follow

yours
Vincent

</HTML>

lost in the translation

In the Song of Oimara
a warrior falls in love with Tavero
but their tribes are at war

Sound familiar?

Oimara can't bear
to be apart from her
so he creeps into Tamarua one night
and hides in a hollow rock

only the set has changed.

He calls to her the next night
on her way back from fishing.
She slips him a fish then a kiss.
This goes on for days

why not a fish?

until someone suspects her
and Oimara is captured
but before they can kill him
he throws himself on the ground
calling her name and dies

those die-hards never learn —
but where's the friar?

Tavero returns to the rock
and sings of her grief
until she can join him
in the spirit world

lost in the translation

if we film It in Hawaii
with Cate and Leonardo
it might just fly

but here it is
more difficult.
And the poem no place
for honesty.

    –John A Scott

when the wandering jew
rises from the ashes
he really is the phoenix

he understands at last
there is no such thing
as absolute land

no matter how big the island
the mind still surrounds itself
instinctively with tides
and the children you have left
are broken shells on the beach

liquid and solid —
it comes down to that
except for fire
and other automatic myths
of purification

circumcision without pain
is possible for the very young
before they understand the pillow

of anaesthetic and how we depend on it
to protect our shorelines
against infusion/diffusion

but what about air?
is it only an filler
between question and answer?
yet we trust it to bear our weight
turning pages from hemisphere
to continent to island to atoll

there is no limit to what we
can explore for the sake of art
pushing back the templates
with landing strips
and wondering what the clear water
and rainforest were before
we drop-shadowed their virginity

yet he goes to the Cook Islands
and Tahiti to search for imagery
arrested footprint on the muddy ledge
of what they have become
in translation

naked bodies
hard nipples
black pearls
facing a northerly wind

fabricating lies on singlets

lost in the translation

Some will attack me
for the titles of my paintings.
They will ask 'has he forgotten
that he is French and that his eyes
will always be French no matter
what ideas he tries to capture?'

Well it's the essence of the sound
that I want not the outer sense
and if the sounds I hear are Tahitian
and tantalisingly blurred in rhythm
then why make them imperial
when raw colours speak the best?

Dreamers will hear what they wish —
for instance my *Nave Nave Fenua*
could mean Delightful Land to those
who imagine Tahiti to be an Eden
where no breast is wrinkled with age
and no spines are stooped by disease.

Scholars will say the title is nonsense
something about the pleasure parents
get from their children on a farm
not what a Tahitian would say at all
but they are only jealous of the liberties
I take in my art and would lash me

with the tyranny of the Word.
It's not for them to pay in currency
to be reminded of their slavery
to the typical where pastries
are baked to be gulped not adored.
But this poem is for you not them.

the internet

I'm a prisoner
of the information I'm given.

    –Gareth Evans

I see him every morning on my walk
an old man in pyjamas
barefoot even in the chill
sitting at a desk in an open garage
studying junk mail as if it were science
newspapers as if they were scripture
licking his lips for current affairs
but settling for gossip

the other day a pollster rang
she was young enough
to be his granddaughter
she kept to her script
and had no interest
in the micro-sprinklers
he'd just installed at great
expense she couldn't see
what that had to do with
what he was willing to pay
for cable TV *agree disagree*
strongly agree strongly disagree
those are your only choices

he had to excuse himself midway
his bladder was calling
on the other line
though he told her someone
was knocking on the door

lost in the translation

don't go away I'll be back in a tick
he coaxed the pale stream out
shook his member only once
didn't even bother to flush
but she'd already hung up

strongly agree he told the dog
when she came in for her feed
scanning her for signs of fleas
that's the right answer isn't it?

you're still in your pyjamas
the dog yawned

<HTML>

'Four Wheels and a Blowjob'?
It certainly sells more papers
than 'Caught in Flagrante Delicto'
if you'll excuse my french.

Not that I mind poor Hugh Grant
but that's what you get for trying
to have a life off the silver screen
and he should have known

what life is like in the big city —
We were just cruising the Sunset Strip
for our quota that night (they all look
the same when their jocks are down).

We gave him his moment of pleasure
before we moved in for the sting.
He's on the back seat of this white
BMW thinking of jolly old England

as the darkie (Divine's her tag)
is working into a froth (but finally
has to use her nails to get a rise).
Made me wonder if the poor bugger

would ever get his money's worth
but 'smile you're on Candid Camera'
says Joe (that line *is* growing whiskers)
and Hugh pops up all red in the face

just like in *Four Weddings and a Funeral*
except this time the bell's tolling for *him*.
The hooker does her best by him says
it was lust at first sight and they're almost

engaged while Hugh stutters one better
says he wanted to see what Richard Gere
must have felt like picking up Julia Roberts.
'Like ten million bucks,' says Joe

booking them, 'except *he* kept his
hard-on to himself, now that's a cool dude!'
Yeah, I *know* they say that Cary Grant
loved to wear women's undies

and Clark Gable had to go down
on a few moguls to make ends meet
before one gave him a screen test
for a job well jacked-off but that was then

and this is now. No greasing of palms
with Internal Affairs watching, pal —
'you're for the line-up, eighteen carats
and smile, you're front page news!'

<HTML>

lost in the translation

Day follows day in endless succession
and the years vanish
but Thy sovereignty endures.

   –the *Union Prayer Book*

he'd been in darkness for so long
he mistook the electronic flashes

for the welcoming futon of death
(the mind's tricks during meltdown)

he'd been fondling the stereos
when the earthquake struck Seoul

buckling the department store
and scuttling the pro-logic demo

(the surround sound was so omnipresent)
suddenly he found himself frozen

in a tomb of girders and concrete slabs
and all around were trembling shards

of glass waiting to bar-code him
but his eyes grew accustomed until

he could tell absence from presence
and proclaim the time of day/night

'it was evening and it was morning
the second day' palpating the shape

of his air sac for anything to chew
chancing upon a fillet of cardboard

below his knees the stomach muscles
so easily assuaged 'and it was evening

and it was morning the fifth day'
a sip of stagnant water was a blessing

to his chapped lips and kept delusions
at the fringes what could be the harm

in casting himself a great white bear
curling to doze in an ice cave if that

tricked his blood? then the idea
of voices overhead dampened before

sharpening into words the cacophony
of hunters in pursuit of their prey

he bared his fangs at the first blast
of air the beam of light invading

his lair and he snarled and twisted
as they bore him on the stretcher

a dancing bear for their photo-ops
'and on the ninth day he was shaved'

</HTML>

change of pace

You get off the plane in Papeete
at three a.m. and wander straight
into someone else's idea of paradise

lassoed by the scent of drunken
flowers you might as well be a Texan
for everything you ask for means

dollars and the Polynesian band
is slightly off key but it's the *effect*
you want after you've paid so much

a daisy chain of tanned shapely bodies
murmuring songs to stereo ukuleles
definitely not the patch for *Debbie Does*

Dallas. 'Australia' you say to the hostess
who squints at your voucher and hears
Atlanta or even Arkansas anywhere

they speak American and she wonders
why you didn't opt for Hawaii instead
or dabble in French *before* you left

but it's too late so she forgives you
and points to a bench where you'll wait
to be shuttled to your hotel where jet

lag's a state of mind and the clerk
at reception squints at your passport
as if Australia's another planet

and all you can think of is a shower
and bed so you bark like John Wayne
to speed up the paperwork and say

merci except it comes out more like
mercy but the clerk hands over a key
and says 'have a nice day' (apprenticed

in Disneyland) and you promise to do
your best once your body and mind
are synchronised at which he smiles

(though the idiom flits over his head
like Tinkerbell) and points you to the lift.
But you're in holiday mode — so relax!

At Rarotonga I settled among the Muri
because I'd heard the fishing was good
and you could scoop *ka'i* from the sand
with half a coconut shell and catch prawns
with a snatch line if you were fast enough.

The Muri were a rugged lot, brewing illegal
beer and stealing from each other but easy
to get along with if they accepted you.
So I told them how I'd used a snatch before
to poach salmon, pheasants and hares

from the property of one Colonel de Burgo
until one grey dawn when his daughter
Camilla caught me crouching by a stream.
She had reddish gold hair and misty eyes
that reminded me of the Connemara Hills

change of pace

skin fragrant as roses after a summer shower
a cluster of freckles, and a nasty shotgun
she used to chase me off into the blackberry
brambles with a burst of pellets. They really
liked that part and had to know what came

next so I told them about when I saw her
at a formal dance. Of course, I'd hoped
to see a tender expression in her eyes
when I asked her for a spin on the floor
but she just smiled and whispered in my ear

how lucky I was that she hadn't had heavier
pellets in her gun or I'd have danced
'a pretty jig back then.' I didn't get a turn
and I lost my snatch, but she didn't dob me in.
The Muri acted out that tale again and again

and before long I'd become a local legend.
My canoe was never nicked, and they'd bring
me oranges, fish and grapefruit. The young men
would grin at me thinking they might be rogues
but at least they'd never been shot in the tail.

The sea of this new world is already better
than those of Europe, calmer and with steadier
winds. Surely it is the New World
which is the best of all possible worlds.

    –*Candide*, Voltaire

dear Mette

Those beautiful pieces they carved
in bone, rock and iron wood —
no weight of gold will bring them back.

The police confiscate everything of value
selling them as curios to any collector
who slips them a few francs for beer.

Is it any wonder that so much fury
creeps into my paintings in Papeete?
I etch Marquesan tattoos into *poi* bowls

to preserve these vanishing motifs
but my impressions are a pale fiction
of what has been scattered to the wind.

All things from home disgust me now.
Maybe that's why I made such a botch
of the Bambridge [38] portrait. I decided

to paint just what I saw, though maybe
I took too much pleasure in depicting
her bulbous nose and the wheelbarrow

width of her hips. Her father called it
'a gross caricature' and has refused to pay
the mirror for its reflection. No matter.

I work best under my own commissions.
Should we counterfeit beauty just to pay
the butcher — or sail with our instinct?

Let them say what they want of my work.
The gale does not remember the debris
it stirs or fret about its opinion nor shall I.

Soon there'll be no more spies from France.
I look forward to being regarded as a perfect
savage and have already burnt my clothes

change of pace

to hasten my expulsion from their harbour
except I must save you somehow my darling!
If only I could persuade you to cut loose

the anchor of "civilisation" and join me
in my rustic state. What more would we need
than this infinite supply of fruit and fish?

Yes, it's true that now I frequent the saloons
instead of salons. And once or twice
I've diverted myself with harlots

(thank Vincent for that!) but to me
they're nothing more than coconut shells
on the beach *something* within reach

to take the edge off my missing you.
Yet I may never find a way to be content
in the old world again. Until I do

you'll have to trust that I am still
devoted to you and cannot imagine
ever being otherwise even if you

should decide to spurn me. You are all
I know of love and all I shall ever seek
to know of it. So take these words to bed

and dream of me and how we'll be again
once this hunger subsides and lets me tack
back into your harbour a contented man.

the internet

we keep the cameras rolling
as the mob advances on the acrylic
shields of the gendarme who form
a tight circle like a wagon train
dodging arrows though there's one
John Wayne who grabs the nearest
Tahitian to arrest him in the name
of Jacques Chirac but he can't quite
remember how it's done on film
with sub-titles so he lets his baton
speak for him until he gets decked
from his blind side by a Patrick Henry
who learned all about the subtext
of pressure points from Cambodian
training videos and then they swarm
over him with kicks taking turns
to bray at the camera (in English!)
'give us liberty or give us death!'

the burning and looting comes later —
a Christmas sale with slightly more
broken glass and frazzled tempers
deftly choreographed just in case
any journos are on the graveyard
shift and they pair off for the TVs
stuffing their pockets with CDs
at the checkout even the classical
ones although none would know
Bolero from Baroque so they'll
trade them off like baseball cards
or take them fishing for good luck

change of pace

the morning after they gather
in the streets to stare at the ruins
the broken panes the hissing ashes
and we keep the cameras rolling
but there's not much chop in a wake
so we queue for the next satellite
timeslot to file our report
then it's off to the next
trouble spot an earthquake perhaps
or a nice flood in China to stir up
those farmers still praying for rain

Jacques Chirac?
he's got a gall nuking those atolls
but he'll be yesterday's fishwrap
unless the boycott of their plonk
begins to bite and he ups the ante
to smoking pistols at High Noon
but never mind those repeats
the next round's on me
so what's your poison, mate?

<HTML>

I thought of my dead mum
over Corn Flakes this morning.

The talkshow was sputtering on
about the treachery of microwaves
and mobile phones causing brain
tumours ('point the antenna away
from your head and don't talk
too long') when just as I lifted
my spoon she was there at the table
a stub of a fag hanging from her lips.

Lucky the kids had gone off to school
or they'd swear I was going stranger
when I said 'oh, it's only you.'
She smiled and puffed on the fag
'till it made me think of fire
and brimstone, so I asked her
'hot enough down there for you?'
She said 'you're a pretty one to talk
with your paperback romances
and those hot flush videos.
At least *I* could tell the difference
between life and make-believe!'

I could feel a migraine coming on
'I do the best I can. It's not easy
on a pension with kids, you know!'
She sneered. 'Didn't I tell you
that three's bad luck? But no, you
had to try for a *girl* again. Jack might
have hung on otherwise.' My head
clenched like a fist. 'Excuse me,'
I said, 'but wasn't it *you* who claimed
good cooking keeps a man hooked
longer than sex?' It was her turn
to groan. 'I *meant* to keep him
on simmer not in the freezer!'
I seized the remote control
pressed the "off" and sure enough
she dissolved in the middle of an ad.
The bloke hawking white goods
was a bit of all right so I undressed him
between the frost free fridge promos
and gave him good head.
'I can't give you more than 30%' he gasped. '
'That's OK,' I said, 'but a jolly rogering

change of pace

wouldn't go astray!' It was unprotected
sex all the way and my Corn Flakes
were all soggy by the time I came to
and I thought I *might* give Jack a call after all
but I got stuck into the crosswords
and just couldn't be bothered.
Hot dreams are better any day
and much easier to flush away.
Sorry, what was that you were saying, Mum?

<HTML>

The ultimate high with Happy Hooker
Hypermedia — first let your modems
rub noses and you're off and surfing

You scroll through "what's cool"
clicking on whatever suits your fantasy
and before you can say 'masturbate'

there's a pathway that titillates
For Classical Guys Only. Click again
and two buttons appear: *I know what I want*

or *Give me a helping hand, Big Boy*! You go for
the latter. A Haydn quartet begins to play
and a silky voice prompts you to be graphic

about your naughties then you get to watch
her take shape — short hair, cool grey eyes
and a trim girlish figure (so she can curl up

in your lap on rainy Sundays). You preset
the time for smalltalk for foreplay the place
where you undress her or better yet where

she undresses you runs her tongue lightly
from your lips to your neck to circle and flick
your nipples as her fingers feather your thighs

while she pins you against the wardrobe
and finally gives your prick a welcoming
squeeze before she guides you inside her

and she's oh so snug because she doesn't
do this much after all she was saving herself
for you and the screen dissolves as she flexes

up and down watching you so she can slow
or quicken to keep you below the threshold
and you feel your body surging to that point

of focus that trigger but you forgot to preset
simultaneous so you come to orgasm without
her and her nails draw blood from your back

you're gasping for air as she finishes herself
and you apologise and she says doesn't matter
it's all cool in love and cybersex and besides

it's on *your* Visa not hers. You open your eyes
and the screen croons *thanks for visiting
The Happy Hooker Docking Station and do*

come again! You smile at the pun and sign off.
It's time for bed and you know you'll sleep well.
In the shower you sing 'happy trails to you...'

</HTML>

soaring

soaring

Scoop up the ocean, soar through the sky —
no matter how far you go, you can't touch
their brimming blue. Water's transparent
so is the sky.

    —Ooka Makoto

Poreo's old now
but when I hand her the guitar
she remembers how to play at once
and her touch is lilting as she teases
the unknown songs back the tears
of vanished years when horses drew
carriages along the white dusty roads
and you could see torches flaring
out at sea where midnight canoes
gleaned a silver spray of flying fish.

His name was Tom Wheedle
and they say he was a plausible
young devil who stole her heart
relishing the bounty as his due.
But when she spoke of marriage
he said it could only be sacred
for him in England, so he'd sail there
build them a nice house then send
for her. She waited for months before
she heard he'd crawled back to his wife.
She didn't want to believe it would sit
by the road strumming the songs
they'd sung until she was covered
with white dust and the grit scratched
her eyes. Finally she cut down six green

drinking coconuts [39] to put in her canoe
and paddled for Ngatangaiia Channel
at midnight then drifting out to the open
sea. Orotea and Kau overtook her
at first light but her mind had completely
gone and she'd wander from village
to village humming silently to herself
eating only when it was put to her lips
but the women would wash her
give her a fresh dress and a place
to sleep but Poreo would drift away
as if she were still in that midnight canoe.

After she finishes the song
she turns to me and manages a faint
smile. For an instant the recesses
of her skin fade and she is a willowy
girl again. But she brushes back the hair
from her eyes glances off to the sea
and walks away without a word
leaving the chords to die in me.

it's that moment before dawn
when the colour begins to lift

and the fishermen ready their boats
for *mahi-mahi* [40] waiting 'till the mist

lifts enough for them to follow
the black birds that soar then circle

over a school of fish and the men
work in concert herding their prey

soaring

into the shallow water where a spear
will make quick work of them

now the black birds follow the men
to the dock where they will stand

waist-deep in bloody water to slit
open their catch tossing the entrails

to the waiting birds there used to be
prayers to a suite of gods but Jesus

simplified all that by being a fisher
of businessmen and impeccably French

so there's no point giving thanks
for the sweat of your brow

you do it because there's nothing else
you'd rather do and out there beyond

the reef you are what you're meant
to be what your father and his

father were before whatever *that* was
but you're sure it was worthwhile

and the chef at the Bali Hai sharpens
his knives and prepares thick batter

it's *mahi-mahi* night and he knows
he can count on you for the fixings

later on you'll play your guitar on board
the *Liki Tiki* for honeymooners sipping

mai tais and when they're good
and pissed you'll tell how the gods

of Bora Bora towed this island here
because it was getting too crowded

in paradise and the young brides
will blush at your bronzed muscles

and dream of you as they lie in bed
with their public servant husbands

whose orgasms come and go as quickly
as the tales of those queer Tahitian gods

He is almost naked as I paint him [41]
this man who needs both his arms
to lift the axe leaving a heavy blue
imprint on the silvery sky
before he brings it down to startle
the dead tree into an instant of flame
while the crimson ground absorbs
the shock in its serpentine metallic-
yellow leaves that spell *atua*. [42]

Mid-distance there's a woman
slightly stooped as she folds a net
carefully into her canoe.
There's a quiet rhythm to her work
and this *ta'ata* [43] is in harmony
with the brilliant blue horizon
and the green waves sense it
as they crest against the coral.

soaring

On the lagoon two men set sail
on an outrigger canoe. The breeze
at first licks them like a soft tongue
then swells and tests the fabric
for the symbolism of open sea.

The more you think about a scene
the warmer it gets and the sugar
lingers on your lips.

the internet

And darkness rises from the eastern valleys,
And the winds buffet her with their hungry breath,
And the great earth, with neither grief nor malice,
Receives the tiny burden of her death.

—A D Hope

A mini-series on *A Current Affair* —
a daughter in the talons of anorexia
between the clips for chocolates
and Just Jeans. The girl on parade
is as tall as Elle MacPherson
though she weighs only 25 kilos
and falling but none of the fashions
suit her because she's still too fat
or so her mirror mirror on the wall
chants. And she hates the tubes
she has to wear for the camera
they inject subversive calories
she might as well be on remand
and the mirror says *pluck them out*
but when she does her sentries her

parents whisk her off to Emergency
where the endless loop starts again
between ads for P & O and Pentiums.

Three days later she's shed another
kilo but Ray Martin reads out a plea
from a little girl who says *please eat
your clothes will fit better if you do
and you'll look pretty again so please*
and the star cries and promises to do
her best but it's hard when you're on
automatic pilot and there's an ad
for tampons nipping at your wheels
and nothing matters but who's seducing
whose wife/husband on *Melrose Place*.

<HTML>

she's a powerwalker
and I see her every morning
pounding down the footpath
in skintight flashy gear
flexing her bar bells
earphones on B-105

she might be a genetic engineer
or perhaps a hired gun in portfolios
who name-drops quad speed CDs
like couplets from Shelley
but she's a performance poem
with no stake in immortality

the glass ceiling shatters for her
and in the boardroom the bored
young men wait for her to test

soaring

the air conditioning they've tried
to entice her with golden calves
but there's nothing she doesn't

know about dolby seductions
or the small print on a Jaguar
and she can walk all over mere
blokes sometimes on the spur
of sex as long as *she* gets to pull
the trigger and keep the remote

control to herself but maybe it's
my Hot Tuna cap and Van Gogh
singlet that makes her double-take
then flash a suburban *why not come
and see me sometime* smile and I
might if I could just rhyme this poem

<HTML>

he's reached his melting point
this keeper of soft- and hardware
he's fallen two conversions behind

on several fronts and his floppy
disk drives are in open rebellion
flirting with Jewel whenever

he turns his back and it seems
the crashes have become deliberate
they're Croat and Bosnian in league

against his Serb in untactical retreat
though he puts on a diplomatic face
when his superiors demand a body

count and he proclaims 'the manuals
are at fault' before recording a fresh
diversion on his answering machine

and sneaking a Valium to counter
the programmed caffeine offensive
wondering if God thinks in macros

or has he surrendered his cookies
to the grim hackers of darkness
like a politician in a by-election

</HTML>

reputations

> You can only tell the truth about people
> in fiction. That's why we have fiction.
>
> —Gore Vidal

In Tahiti there are many names
for shark and your life may depend
on knowing which one you face

in the shallows with only a fishing
net to play matador to its jaws.
Slap the water or blow bubbles

and you'll scare the *mauri* away
but a *mamaro* will shrug this off
and still circle while the *raira*

may charge. You may be quick
to haul your catch into the canoe
but it will only infuriate him if

you do not toss him a tribute
before casting in your net again.
Never mistake a blunt snout

for stupidity. He will sense this
and worry you until you swamp.
You will know you are in trouble

when he lowers his pectoral fin
and shakes his head. But nothing
will prepare you for a *mao tore tore*. [44]

Pure fury he will charge anything
that dares to infringe his territory.
We catch him with a slab of pig meat

baited on a big hook tied to a steel
cable lashed to a coconut palm.
Slashing him open we have exposed

sea birds turtles and small sharks
even a goat but his flesh is tender
and worthy of hot coals. Taste him?

dear Mette

It was lonely for me on Mataiea
so I asked Titi to come from Papeete.
She had to leave behind a young officer
who tempted her with perfume and silks.
Maybe she thought I wanted to paint her
again as I did in *Te faaturuma* [45]

but I'd already captured her essence
and only wanted her frame to play on.
With those thighs and muscular calves
she has a vitality that has been drained
from our women yet she's no longer
that savage of silent beauty I drew

and must be entertained and flattered
with French cliches. She finds me boring
which is the only thing that suits me
about her now and she insists on silverware
rather than her fingers to linger
over the pleasures of food.

While I listen to *himenes* [46] she scuffs along
the beach. It saddens me to think how little
time it took to pollute her and sadder still
when I realise it was I who first tempted her
with the tainted produce of civilisation.
I can't endure these charades any more

so I've sent her packing. She went quite happily
saying anyway I look much better in a white suit
than a pareu. Perhaps we do not age like wine
and what we call experience is only a fiction
we use to appease our impertinent shadows.
I haven't mentioned Titi? Well, I *meant* to.

They tell the best stories down at the bar.
One was about this randy sheep farmer
from Montana who'd scrimped for years

for a glimpse of paradise. When this girl
waited on him it was lust at first sight
so he offered to buy her a fancy dress

if she'd nuzzle his fantasies for a night.
She showed him such a good time
sucking his fingers and licking his toes

that he promised to give it all away
to make an honest woman of her
but she said she'd prefer the dress.

He got stroppy then so she nicked
his dentures to play Carmen dancing
on the bar with castanets for her drinks

Letters We Never Sent

then she flung them into the lagoon.
He called her a slut and filed a claim
for the loss on his insurance that he won

for originality. He went back to Montana
with a new lease on life. After all he'd seen
paradise and it was no crate of cherries

was it? The sheep gave him no sympathy.
'The Cook Islands? That ain't *our* notion
of the Second Coming — serves you right!'

the internet

A simplification of means
and an elevation of ends
is the means.

    –Thoreau

they say we get the Demidenkos we deserve

a darling of the multi-culturally correct —
the publicist could hardly believe her luck:
female (of course), blond hair to her bum
(a subliminal haystack for potential male
readers), a nice slash of thigh (to keep
the lesbians keen) and a virtual reality
that forces the reviewers to eulogy

we have found her
a Joan of Arc in Brisbane
who will spur the tropos

*into their first golden age
and the Literature Board
will forsake Sydney for Noosa*

*and grants will fall like manna
from a pristine sky and no one
will talk of drought any more*

she wears her dyslexia like a badge
(it hardly shows!) and outs an illiterate
father who drives a taxi in Cairns (how's
that for humid interest?), not to mention
half-Ukrainian (a latter-day Solzhenitzen?),
but there's more to this twenty-four carat

(clasp those statements of account!)
a dux from a private girl's who topped it
in maths who was summoned to the bar
only to find it tedious and who wasn't afraid
to quote the Talmud back at bleeding-heart
rabbis who see atrocities in black and red
(take that, Stendhal, you has-been!)
the first chapter almost brought me to tears
so I put the rest on my list when the Vogel
landed and I swear I *would* have finished it
when the Miles Franklin judges capitulated
if I hadn't had those blasted press kits

to write. I was thinking why *not* a Booker
when the storm hit the wires — Darville?
You could have blown me over with a Sao
when her boyfriend spilled the plagiarism
and her headmaster brandished the mugshot
and someone started a rumour about The Hand

That *Forged* The Paper — the unkindest cut
of all! So we slipped into damage control
and went half and half with her on a QC
to blind the sharks with writs. Which finally
gave me time to finish the book and see what
a crock it was — though she knew how to dot her i's.

We *do* get the Demidenkos we deserve
I suppose, but who was it said truth's sweeter
than fiction? Not this bruised babe!

\<HTML\>

Spare some change for poor Christopher Skase
our frail tall poppy going to seed on Mallorca.
He'd certainly come back home if only someone
would shout him a business medico flight.
He's done his sums on the Serra de Tramuntana [47]
and found there's no future in charcoal burning
or Iberian fleshpots — after all you can only
keep the thornbush hacked back for so long
before your fingers say *enough of limestone
and olive pits there must be more to life
than this litany of bankrupt sunsets!*

He's been sighted everywhere but here:
in London at the Last Night of the Proms
puffing on his ventilator before burying
his face in the sweaty bosom of a would-be
alto; in Berlin to consecrate the Euro
before trekking off in a NATO tank bound
for Sarajevo; exchanging hallucinations
with Michael Jackson aboard a mystery
flight to the Antarctic in a fund-raiser
for vertically challenged Emperor Penguins;

and most recently in Hong Kong where he
autographed copies of his latest how-to book
Measured Breathing Can Change Your Life.

All of this is true and more —
Nelson Mandela has him on retainer
Boris Yeltsen's memorised his fax number
John Major's bought the motivational video
and Bill Clinton buggers his hairdresser.
But our hero's homesick and tired of flogging
the Sydney Harbour Bridge to menopausal
Kentucky Fried heiresses from Houston
for cashflow and he doesn't get Christmas
cards from Toorak now so I ask you
WHAT'S THE POINT?!

Why not charter a jumbo
and a few hacks from the AMA
put him on Red Faces with Bob Hawke
(who can shed the biggest crocodile tears?)
then baptise a university in memoriam
or rename a theme park (how does
Skaseworld on the Sunshine Coast
strike you?) after all the only brake
on creativity is your overdraft
when you hail from a clever country.

There! I've started things off with a legit
fifty dollar note. Now the top hat's come
round to you. Cash only of course (the more
liquid the better) and no American Express
or Diner's Club please (the money trail's scent
is too strong). He'll make us a fortune
in no time — just you wait and see —
or my name's not Paul Keating

(or is that John Howard?) Never mind
that landfill of creditors over there
just make out your cheque to our next
Prime Minister and you'll be right.

As an act of good faith Christopher
has promised to donate two cents
on every dollar to asthma research
so if you can't trust a philanthropist
who can you trust? Give generously
and often.

<HTML>

He brought Bach to the wilderness
this man [48] who had to trust his piano
to a hollowed-out tree when God called him

across the sea to a land that devoured
its own children. Back in Alsace
he'd made his mark as a brilliant

musician though not the sinew of myths.
'Who can be content with art,' he said,
'when every note you hear is a dirge

to a Dark Land's despair?'
He named his code *reverence for life*
refused to harm even a fly

and pretended not to notice when others
began to shape his words into a statue.
In Lambaréné he washed the feet of lepers

but when they compared him to Christ
he thrice refused the crown of thorns.
'Jesus was just a good man,' he claimed

reputations

'and I can be no less in my mission to undo
the power of superstition.' So he ministered
to the sick and stirred the conscience of those

God protects in war or in the tedium of peace
when the urge for sanctity seems peripheral
to the fight to stay awake. And when the disciples

came to declare him Man of the Century
he wore a bow tie for them so that the world
would not think any less of him for his sacrifice.

'I never doubted that fame would come to me,'
he confessed, 'and I want my life to continue
just as it is until I die.' He preferred to feed

a man a fish than to teach him how to catch it.
But Africa refused to hold his pose. Black men
began to master white medicine in the vacuum

and no one bothered to tell him he'd outlived
his sainthood. The letters of adulation slowed
to a trickle then changed to recriminations.

He put this down to the caprices of fashion —
what did *they* know about conquering shadows
or orchestrating a chorus of light? He died

in the hospital he loved encircled by a host
of starched nurses who would make a shrine
of this man who was famous for being good

even after he slipped from gold into bronze
by insisting the world should perform as he
composed it — a requiem not an anthem.

</HTML>

Letters We Never Sent

keepsakes

The poem, consigned
and claimed, deepening in sand,
shifting, reaches among layers
to a beginning, to ends...

    –Judith Rodriguez

Can you imagine the moment of a blood-seed?
Vairaumati [49] has told Oro that she is pregnant
by him. He has left to sacrifice a pig at the great
marae leaving her alone. To her left is a bowl
of ripened mangoes, behind her two mountains
give birth to a valley. Her lips are still moist

with words but no one is there to listen. While
you carry the spark for future generations
you must contain it — that is the burden
of immortality. So it was for Mary, and Isis
denounced by candles at St. Germain-des-Prés [50]
also Lord Buddha, forced to smile as monks

bathed his feet. What matters is the aftermath
of coupling, those fertile moments of half-sleep
before lovers lapse into the lock-step of jade,
when colours confess their part in the image
feeding the relentless cascade of the primitive.
I let those waters refresh me and am content.

Was there ever a man as wretched
as Te-Pou-o-te-Rangi?
His wife died in childbirth
so he was left to raise his little girl.

keepsakes

As chief of Avarua he could have had
any woman but he'd buried his spirit
with Tioro. And now his greatest fear
was that Veena might also be lost.

He brought young Teina to his house.
'You'll prosper here,' he promised,
'so long as you guard my little jewel
with your life. But fail and you shall die.'

Teina had a dream about him.
She'd care for his daughter so well
that in time he might come to love her.
And she would bear him a son
who would be chief in his turn
But that was not to be.

One day Teina took Veena to the beach.
Her plan was to fish in the shallows
of the lagoon in her father's canoe.
She cushioned the floor with coconut fronds
and swaths of grass for the girl to sleep on
then set off. It was a cloudless afternoon
and the sun danced off a thousand mirrors.

As Teina swirled the water with her net
she dreamt of how marvellous it would be
when Te-Pou-o-te-Rangi wakened to her.
But the breeze swung them out beyond
the reef and the swells had caught the boat
before Teina saw the danger and paddled
for shore with all her might. Veena clung to her
with wild animal eyes as the canoe fell away
to the open sea.

They drifted for five days and nights.
Teina fed Veena the flesh and milk
of the green coconuts she'd brought along
and shaded the child from the sun's glare
with her body. She could feel her own skin
cracking and blistering as she grew weaker.
In her delirium she saw Te-Pou-o-te-Rangi
paddling furiously at her through a choking
fog. 'My Veena!' he shouted. 'You must die
for this!' Suddenly he became a tiger shark
and swamped the canoe. 'I loved you!'
she cried before his teeth crushed her chest
and her blood lashed out onto the dark waves.
'I loved---'

They were rescued by two Atiu fishermen
and before she died Teina begged them
to return Veena to her father. Their chief
would have none of it since his people
and the Rarotongans were still at war.
He saw no reason why the death-rattle
of a nursemaid should change that.
Meanwhile, Te-Pou-o-te-Rangi became
a broken and embittered man and the people
spoke softly in his presence. Every night he'd sit
on the beach, gazing out beyond the reef.
No one dared to disturb him. He ruled
like that for sixteen years while the hatred
between the Atiuans and his people gradually
cooled. One day a fleet of Atiuan canoes
were spotted off shore. Te-Pou-o-te-Rangi
ordered his men to don their war helmets
but then they saw green coconuts lashed
to the bow of each boat — a sign of peace.

keepsakes

From the leading boat stepped Veena
wearing a *tia* made from pearl and dressed
in the robes of a princess. Te-Pou-o-te-Rangi
did not know her until she wrapped her arms
around him and called him father. What a feast
there was then! The people were at peace
and Te-Pou-o-te-Rangi renamed his family
Vakatini. [51] He built a memorial to Teina
on a rocky outcrop overlooking the sea
and draped it with flowers on the holy days.
He never remarried. 'Two women died for me,'
he said. 'That's more than enough for any man.'

It was a strange place, the Gauguin museum.
In the newer section, none of his work at all

forgettable acrylics by a flash-in-the-pan artist
with cryptic glosses in Japanese and German

or English — if you knew how to ask for them
in French. The guide said we could commission

variations to suit our furnishings if price
were no object. I said our walls were all taken

and besides modern art left us rather cold.
So she left for brighter prospects, a half-circle

of Germans ogling a swirl of thighs and tits.
I wondered what this had to do with Gauguin

whose work was cramped on tacky white brick
open to the garden, with no air conditioning

or synthesised music to tempt my credit cards.
First I looked at his self-portrait, unframed.

This was Europe, not Tahiti — I wanted the savage
who'd sold his birthright for a pareu and traded

his wife for nymphs who'd worship his pale skin.
Other canvases were cracked from the salty air.

Women in starched caps gather the wheat
a farmer wonders what the season will bring

besides the pigs snuffling at his feet. Very few
Tahitian scenes, the best having leached away

and fallen under the hammer for a fortune.
No respect here for what an exile endured

to hone his genius. No sense of narrative
or counterpoint between what he thought

he'd find and the balm of a sleepy hibiscus.
Still, the tourists genuflect to these ruins

without complaint and what they discover
or miss as they promenade doesn't matter

as long as they buy a trinket on their way out:
take pride in a still life judiciously framed

wipe your hands for fertility on a tea-towel
of *Vairaumati Tei Oa* or forage for pillow slips

of matched *arioi*. Then again a key chain portrait
of the Master himself might be a safer keepsake

(never be locked out of your Peugeot again!)
Now that packaging's the game soon there'll be

keepsakes

Gauguin the Rock Musical followed by the film
starring an emaciated Gerard Depardieu

(courtesy of Weight Watchers). But who'd
have thought they'd *all* be nipped at the wire

by a poet of the virtually real who says it all
without resorting to rhyme for a mere $17.95?

the internet

The flying fish have returned to the creek
which has been dry since my daughter
was born. Drought has a way of insisting
through wasted earth through choirs
of locusts. Blue skies, a tone poem sun —
melodies revisited become a torture
scribbled off the page. When I was young
we stole love in the winter wheat.
Were cracked lips to be my penance?

But now the flying fish have returned
with the rain and the brown water
that swells the banks under the bridge
and my daughter poses there between
spurts of green her hair gone all curly
with the teasing humidity. She dances
for me though she is too young to know
the significance of soaking rain the deathroll
of despair. And I am thinking of you again
despite my covenant with Christ our Lord.

Can you taste my tears?

\<HTML\>

Letters We Never Sent

My father's house was razed
in nineteen forty-eight
when the Israelis passed
over our street.

The house was built of stone
and had a small courtyard
where, on a hot day, one
could sit in shade

under a tree and have
a glass of something cool.
Friendship rose like a wave
from our deep well

and no one was turned away.
The doorstep soon wore down.
Now I see in my mind's eye
an aching crescent moon.

Of that house, not a wall
in which a bird might nest
was left to stand. Israelis
laid it all to waste.

Though we must pay to drink
our water, and our wood
is sold back to us, we thank
Allah the supreme God.

Let the supplanter choke
upon his harvest. Our faith
will take the stones he broke
and break his teeth. [52]

\<HTML\>

keepsakes

I was born a year before that
when Israel was still a dream
and the Holocaust a nightmare.

We lived in a land of freedom
safe from the flare of pogroms.
They called it Middle America

and our houses were made of brick.
At twilight my father sat with me
on the front steps hosing our lawn

until his heart failed. Then my mother's
paranoia bloomed. Who could she blame
for the dead grass? The panzer demons

had fled to hell and her mother
had worshipped Lenin and Marx
so who was left to drive into the sea

but the Palestinian hordes? For years
they were maggots to me unworthy
of life. What God could be bothered

to proxy them? But I have since seen
what bitterness breeds when a people
resurrect their pride and it makes me

want to denounce their Promised Land
for the unholy fortress it has become.
If double-agents broadcast my purpose

I won't deny them. I kick off quickly
from shore and paddle for that atoll
where narrow gods are strictly taboo.

I carry no luggage but my theosophy
and the people take me as their own —
while my mother sleeps underground.

<HTML>

The hardest thing was to accept
it could have been one of our own
who shot him. Grown men cried
'One Jew assassinate another —
how could such a horror be?

and a pillar of fire was seen
above the camp

Rabin stood there on the platform
floating on a lagoon of his supporters
and in words he was more a rabbi
than a prime minister. 'Let the sun
rise, and mornings light our way.'

from the swirl of flames a voice

His happiest hour, his wife recalled
in the synagogue, eyes clear and dry
while candles still flared in the square.
Heroic in war and martyred in peace —
who could ask for a better epitaph?

ashes were thy name
but now thou art reborn
with the sinews of Sampson
and the wisdom of Solomon

A million tongues swore to bury us
by the sword by machine gun by hard

labour and they threw us in the pits
where a slurry of clay and effluent
wedded our flesh to gipsies.

disarmed is dismembered

*look to Joshua to steel thy children
by striking fear in the hearts of those
who would annihilate thy blood*

Now we are a confident nation again
because of the vision of men like Yitzhak.
But it is an angry forest that we plant
in the soil of war and there are those
who would keep us an island on edge.

*your enemies will chew the bones
of your philosophy*

only force breeds respect

We must fight all the harder to cement
this peace to cast off the centuries of hate
and distrust. Our children must believe
that a state always at war feeds on itself.
We must give voice to a fresh vocabulary.

*they shall speak of the glory of thy kingdom
and talk of thy might*

</HTML>

twilight of the gods

The fire still burns there.
Send logs to Valhalla.

    –Richard Wagner

dearest Mette,

After the king [53] died they laid him in an admiral's
uniform in his palace for all to see. It saddened me
to have come so far to witness the passing
of the splendour he had come to symbolise
and the inevitable triumph of the new ways
over the old. Soon there will be nothing more
than "civilisation" here. The *marae* have all
fallen into decay, and what the rapacious weeds
do not smother, scurrilous farmers cart away
at night to fence their cattle, pigs and chickens.

When I painted *Arii Matamoe* [54] I knew
my figures would be butchered by those
who think my appreciation of Tahitian motifs
naive. You must tell them they are wrong.
It's true that the natives are not in the habit
of decapitating their kings to preserve them
for posterity on white pillows or otherwise
but my concept is larger than these islands. [55]
How else should I rail against the usurpers
who debilitate these cultures by degree?

On nights like this when the stars
burn down on me I feel I should return
to you before I lose what threads still bind me
to what I thought of as home. But then I can't

twilight of the gods

deny the sense that I *belong* here
and must persist until I have reached
the far shore of my primitive nature.

How can I give in to either voice?
By giving in to one wouldn't I grow
the more restless for the other?

I have shed my skin so many times
that the raw flesh may terrify you.
Perhaps there is affection in distance
after all. Who's to say that an embrace
is better than an intimate turn of brush
or a chorus transposed into a letter
only meant for your ears?

If only I could afford to bring you here to see
my precious garden, society might pale for you.
But that is not to be, just as I cannot return
before I finish. I must be what I'm becoming —
a happy slave to the spice of inspiration.
Once the future's promise is on our tongue
we must pursue until we make it our own!

Why did I choose to marry, then?
Love must be a part of all we do.
But there must be more to it than a threat
of stone else we go stale. Without art
there's no fertility. And true love does not
test the bond of those who must divide
their attention. We must have infinite patience.

We are apart yet undivided.
Separation makes us all the stronger
our devotion to reunion more determined

Letters We Never Sent

though I know it must be harder for you
than it is for me. And so I'll make it up to you
in paint if not words because you believe in me
and are with me in my struggle for the grail.

Faith.
Vision.
Hard work.
Realisation.

A west wind blows down
from the central mountains.

It means good fishing on the reef
so why am I here alone?

The tides are restless
teeming with hungry jaws.

Thigh-deep I wade across the lagoon
to the glistening white beach on Koromiri
then on to the sighing brown-backed reef
washed with lazy wavelets and there are
cormorants sandpipers and a fine shoal
of *kanae* leaping in the blue water ahead.

It was the same the day I landed
but tomorrow may change all that.

The sun sets behind the darkening peaks
and along the curving stretch of reef
there are no fishermen in frayed hats
or girls in bright *pareus* with buckets of bait
no children splashing in the shallows

twilight of the gods

no voices calling each to each
no canoe to lean on as you roll a cigarette
and gaze at the motionless palm trees
and the reef steadily disappearing
under the gleaming curves of tide.

No one's in sight.
No lilting voices from the pews.
No guitars strumming island songs.
They are glued to radios now
and deluged by American tunes
even as their rhythms vanish.

I was the future when I came
but now I am the present.

Undertaker for the mute.

The lagoon is lonely now.
Oti ra ua.

You shall blow the trumpets
over your burnt offerings
and the peace offerings...

    –Numbers, 10

our last night on Moorea
we walked from the Bali Hai
to the Itchy Dragon for dinner

it wasn't the done thing
and people stared as they cruised past
in their tinted rental cars

sunset wasn't particularly grand —
I'd expected longer would be better
but the reds just dwindled to grey
(there's something to be said
for the Aussie quickie after all!)

the restaurateur was French
the word was that he'd deserted ship
for a fling with a Tahitian woman
who had a way with Chinese cuisine
and other more intimate pastimes
that made the routine that was Paris
seem like yesterday's fish wrapping

their kitchen was definitely kitsch
(a Renault van he'd disembowelled)
and their sink was in a feral canoe
but the tamarind duck was brilliant
and you could see that he'd achieved
harmonic resonance with fried rice
and fraternity on a bamboo skewer

he spoke about France and the things
he didn't miss — the politics, the hot
pursuit of *things*, the pretence of art —
after our first bottle the house red
and conversation was on him
and we'd have come back for more
except our itinerary was fixed
and I felt a cyclone coming on

it was moonless on the road
but the stars rhapsodic
as I stretched out to them
thinking of poor Vincent

twilight of the gods

who'd have gone the distance here
if he and Gauguin had patched it up

I imagine him camping on the beach
making do on overripe fruit and crusts
imagining the occasional croissant
Paul would shout him when they
were having a sunflower day at the palette

he might have kept his ear to himself
flirting in the shade with native sheilas
taking each afternoon like the next
on a hammock with a rum and bitter
willing fortune to discover him

looking forward to night and the calming
of the tides in his mind if only he'd known
how to lift the window shade on turmoil
and found an island refuge such as this
he *might* have soldiered on for our sake

but the maze stumped him
so I must address this to a rusted
post box somewhere in the sticks
where unfinished symphonies wait
for genius to be endowed once again

meanwhile along our night path
the Adventists are seeding the humid air
with hymns like *trust in Jesus for He is strong*
and we could have been in Alabama
or Natal Province or even Bethlehem

evangelists have such a long half life
and faith grows stronger the more remote

you are from the blood-soaked crossroad
though the wafers taste of plastic
praise Him praise His Holy

offshore a great cruise ship anchors
her sails drenched with floodlights
she is commerce *praise his Holy Name*
and offers her best profile for syndication
soon she'll be clip art on the internet

a bitmap of her former self unless a Jupiter
plots her vectors into animated 3-D for kicks
praise Him enhances her into a supermodel
snuggles her into hypertext then launches her
across the face of the world wide web

the more things change
the faster they change

praise

GOD :Noah, how long can you tred water?

    —Bill Cosby

our last night on Aitutaki 56
it began to bucket down
you took that as an omen
that we'd stayed too long

and now the only question was
how long it would take the dove
to cash in her shares on the ark
and hitch onto a high speed cat

twilight of the gods

the staff tried to remain cheerful
as a cunning stream began to wind
through reception to the cocktail lounge
then out toward the salt water pool

(divide and conquer?) 'the next round's
on the house' the manager declared
and we dutifully cheered/queued up
and ordered another piña colada

I offered a toast to Ronald Symes
whose book I'd found almost by chance
in a dusty stack at the university library
no one at the bar had heard of his prose

they measured their nights in swizzle-sticks
ending in a return doze back to their jobs
with no worries of how lonely the lagoon
might have been for some born-again journo

of course the lagoon hadn't missed him
toggling from turquoise shallows to azure
seductive as ever under the shimmering sun
singularly unimpressed by the reconstituted

missionaries and tourists who'd flared
and fizzled since his thoughts dilated
bequesting a buoy to the British Museum
to be catalogued with the grumpy stonefish

meanwhile the monsoon was getting bolder
and the clouds darkening to apocalypse
our baggage struggled for higher ground
while the manager put on a practiced face

'neither winds nor hail nor torrents
can deter Air Rarotonga' he intoned
winking at us because he preferred
Aussies to Yanks (islanders *understand*

that the gods can be abrupt and adjust
their native theologies accordingly)
but his bravado didn't convince you
so I said 'God looks after his own'

'whose God?' you replied 'whose own?'
I suppose you had a point — how many
chosen can there be before a conflict
of interest sets in? how can a dove

draw the line between the politician
who bump-and-grinds his orthodoxy
and the zealot who kills for the sake
of eternal principles? it's a refuge

for wanderers who try to write poems
or paint or simply connect with *someone*
on the world wide web of intercourse
as you did for me Ron — so here's to you!

the bus arrives to take us to the airstrip
and the manager crosses himself in jest
then the storm pulls out all the stops
so our odyssey will climax properly

you cling to me as the plane accelerates
and streams of water obscure the glass
but the takeoff goes pretty well considering
the pilot wasn't Greek or even an islander

twilight of the gods

after we're above the clouds I fancy myself
as Ulysses taking shape in Homer's mind
sailing home heavy with the diaries of fate
to dream perchance to reconstruct

and I *know* I'll have to write it all down
for the sake of the past present and present
past and launch it into cyberspace our next frontier
where imagination's tall ship has already set sail

References

[1] Herman Melville, seeing Tahiti-nui for the first time.

[2] Gauguin's wife, who stayed behind in Paris with their two children.

[3] Ronald Syme, The Lagoon Is Lonely Now.

[4] on Rarotonga, Cook Islands.

[5] shellfish.

[6] Reverend William Gill.

[7] 'by dint of always wanting to be at the forefront,' Gauguin wrote, 'he has lost every scrap of personality and his entire body of work lacks unity.'

[8] William McBirney's retelling of the myth of Te Ana Takitaki (The Cave To Which One Was Led).

[9] a sacred place, outdoors.

[10] cliff.

[11] a small bird with scarlet feathers, used in a chief's headdress, now extinct.

[12] pride, bravado.

[13] a member of the "Bounty" crew.

[14] priests.

[15] the shark gods.

[16] Long live the king!

[17] sorry.

[18] another artist, who left Tahiti four days before Gauguin arrived.

[19] a television quiz show that was eventually shown to be rigged, with Van Doren, who'd had the nation spell-bound up to that point as the most successful prize-winner, admitting he'd been supplied the answers in advance.

[20] She Is Thinking of the Spirit of the Dead.

[21] Gauguin's daughter, who died of pneumonia in Copenhagen while he was still in Tahiti. She never read the notebook, Cahir pour Aline, which Gauguin had dedicated to her.

[22] spears.

[23] road.

[24] a tribe of Indians in Northern Alberta.

[25] nobility.

[26] Van Gogh, who died less than two years before.

[27] about five francs.

[28] a novel by Edmond de Goncourt.

[29] I am of sound mind, I am the Holy Ghost.

[30] after the satiric romance Tartarin de Tarascon by Alphonse Daudet; the Midi is a region in southern France known for its braggarts, and Tartarin, who was best known for his garden of exotic plants, is forced to travel to Africa to prove his boasts of being of lion tamer. Atelier = workshop.

[31] the young Van Gogh had completed theological studies and was intent on saving the poor.

[32] his brother.

[33] Anthon van Rappard (1858-92), a Dutch painter, with whom Van Gogh broke off his friendship after the former criticised this painting as being based on figures who were 'only posing'.

[34] the work of Adolphe Monticelli (1824-86), whose technique gave free rein to intense colour and texture in his painting, inspired Van Gogh to come to Arles.

[35] Gauguin, who stayed with him in Arles for a few trying months.

[36] where he read Henry V while painting this canvas.

[37] this painting celebrated the birth of Theo's son, whom he named after his brother, saying '[m]y wish is that he will have the same perseverance and will be just as courageous as you.'

[38] Susanne Bambridge, the only commission Gauguin managed to complete in Tahiti, though he claimed he'd been asked to paint many more.

[39] a ritual means of suicide.

[40] a large fish, considered a delicacy.

[41] L'Homme à la hache (Man with an Axe), painted in 1891 on the island of Moorea.

[42] god.

[43] person, though the word reminded Gauguin of Thagata, Buddha in the aspect of achieving Nirvana.

[44] tiger shark.

[45] Silence or Mournful Spirit.

[46] Hymn-singing.

[47] a mountain ridge on the island, but also the name of the north-west wind that howls in the winter.

[48] Albert Schweitzer.

[49] from the creation myth of arioi society, a goddess who becomes the wife of Oro before he has asked her name, who Gauguin depicts in his painting Te Aa No Areois.

[50] a statue of Isis was kept in the church here until it was noticed that women were mistaking her for the Virgin and burning candles to her.

[51] many canoes.

[52] the 'Chorus of Exiled Palestinians', Klinghoffer.

[53] Pomare V. Gauguin saw his death as a metaphor for the death of Tahitian culture.

[54] The Death of Royalty.

[55] Gauguin likely based the image on a moko mokais from the Maori of New Zealand who did follow the practice of preserving not only the heads of royalty but also those of their enemies.

[56] one of the Cook Islands.

Interactive Press showcases the best modern literature by Australian authors. Publishing digital as well as print texts, IP seeks to promote and market its work to the widest possible audience.

For further information, please contact:

Interactive Publications
9 Kuhler Court
Carindale, Queensland, Australia 4152
Phone/fax (business hours): 61 7 3395-0269
Mobile: 0412-313923
info@interpr.com.au
http://www.interpr.com.au/titles.htm

Recent Titles

Hemingway in Spain and Selected Poems by David P Reiter, 1997, ISBN 0 646 327 46 1, PB, 192 pp, RRP $17.95. Shortlisted for the John Bray Award at the 1998 Adelaide Festival Literary Awards.

Old Time Religion and Other Poems by Andrew Leggett, 1998, ISBN 1 876819 00 6, PB, 112 pp, RRP $17.95. 'His method is confrontational, his insights acute.' – Judith Rodriguez.

Bermuda and the Other Islands by Juliana Burgesen-Bednareck, 1998, ISBN 1 876819 01 4, PB, 152 pp, RRP $17.95. 'The poems crackle with immediacy, suppleness and vision.' – Katherine Gallagher.

Triangles by David P Reiter, 1999, ISBN 1 876819 03 0, PB, 216 pp, RRP $18.95. Stories of our time from a multi-award winning author – the loves we dream of as opposed to the relationships that define us.

Facing the Pacific by Michael Sariban, 1999, ISBN 1876819 02 2. 'Sariban catches the unexpected moment in alert, memorable language.' – Thomas Shapcott.

A Deep Fear of Trains by Sara Moss, 2000. ISBN 1876819 05 7. In this brash first collection, Moss strips complacency away from the poetic experience.